Touche
(The Touch Series, #3)
By t.h. snyder

Heather,
everyone deserves
a second chance
at love!

♥ th snyder

© 2014 t. h. snyder (Tiffany Snyder)

Published by t. h. snyder

First published in 2014. All rights reserved. This book is copyright. Apart from the fair purpose of private study, research or review as permitted by the Copyright Act, no part may be reproduced without written permission.

This book is licensed for your personal enjoyment only. This book may not be re-sold or given away to other people. If you would like to share this book with another person, please purchase an additional copy for each recipient. If you're reading this book and did not purchase it, or it was not purchased for your use only, then please return and purchase your own copy. Thank you for respecting the hard work of this author.

This is a work of fiction. Names, characters, places, and incidents are the product of the imagination or are used fictitiously. Any resemblance to actual, locales or persons, living or dead, is entirely coincidental.

Images Copyright

Book Cover By Design: Kellie Dennis

Acknowledgements

I want to THANK the following people for their SUPPORT and ENCOURAGEMENT throughout this journey.

My family! Mom (Roberta), Angie, Dad and Mar, you guys CHEER me on every day telling me how PROUD you are of my ACCOMPLISHMENT. I couldn't have done this without you and all your love and support.

To my two WONDERFUL kids, you are my world Raeghyn, and Mason. I love you both to infinity and beyond

My FANTASTIC writing BFF's. The three of us have come so far in such a short time. I'm proud of the ways in which we've grown and can't believe what we've accomplished in six months. I love you both....Traci and Trisha #thisishappening!!!

My BETA GIRLS! You've stuck with me and I'm honored to have you all by my side throughout this journey. No matter how stupid I think a chapter may be, these girls are my rocks....love you Amy Conception, Jennifer Maikis, Crystal Rearick, Barb Johnson, Joanne Schwehm, Karrie Puskas and Yamara Martinez.

Kellie Dennis, you are my ROCKSTAR and I love what you've done with this cover. It is absolutely beautiful.

Tiffany Tillman, you blew my mind with your amazing edits and input, I love you and glad to have you as part of my dynamic team.

Christine Stanley you are more than just a friend and support system to me, you are a part of my family. I love you hard girl. We are stuck together so tight that at times I think we share a brain.

My SPICE GIRLS…wow, I think we know way too much about one another, but without you girls my life would be empty. Love y'all long time Kathy Coopmans, Karrie Puskas, Nikki Flannery, Heather Slayton and Yamara Martinez.

A special shout out to a few authors that I know and LOVE very much. Without your support and encouragement, I'd be lost. I love you Margaret McHeyzer, Joanne Schwelm, Trudy Stiles, Michelle Polk and Julie Morgan.

Prologue

After ten years of marriage, I can't believe things are happening the way they are between us. When we said our vows all those years ago, I imagined it would be forever. I never thought I'd be in the situation I am right now.

I sit here staring out the huge bay window in our living room. This is our home; the place we built for us and our future family.

Who would've ever known we would eventually fall apart, become broken and the dreams of that perfect family would never really happen?

I sink into the soft brown leather couch that faces the front yard and think of when we first found this lot of land—the visions I had of our perfect life. Now looking back, I realize how stupid and naïve I really was to think it would all work out as planned.

I wonder if other married women have felt the way I'm feeling right now.

It's not deceit. I've never been disloyal to my husband. *He's* the one who's been leading a life of lies.

I shake my head at the thought of it and close my eyes.

Years of hurt and pain fly through my mind and I wish I could take back some of the things I've done or said to those that were closest to me.

I honestly can't say that it's entirely his fault though; I've been leading a life of lies as well.

I've been hiding from reality.

I wanted things to appear perfect on the outside, but that's only because I had to be the perfect wife.

Opening my eyes, I don't know how much longer I can keep up this charade.

I see his truck pull up the bottom of the driveway and exhale the breath in my lungs I must've been holding.

Is it wrong for me to hate that he's home?

Does it make me a bad wife that I'm beginning to feel sick?

Will others judge me when they find out the truth behind the lies we've been keeping?

I stand up from my couch and grasp my hands together as I walk toward the kitchen.

I get myself into a cluster fuck of emotion every time I know he's going to be near me. It affects me so greatly that my nerves are a jumbled mess.

Once I confront him, if I choose to go through with it, everything will be different. I'm not sure if it will explode in my face or if it will be the closure we need to go our separate ways. I *do* know that something needs to happen. *Now.* I have to tell him that I know what he's been doing this whole time.

I can't let him continue to torture me the way he has for the past few weeks… months….wait, no, years.

No matter how hard it will be, I have to stand up for me, my family and my future.

I deserve better.

I want to be happy again.

I'm worth so much more than the life he's taken away from me.

Part 1

My Life Before You

I was living a life where there was no happiness;

desperate to find that one person

who would make me feel whole again.

Chapter 1

Friday February 3, 2012

Emma

I'm nervous as hell as Keith and I walk toward the doctor's office.

He lets go of my hand for a brief second as he opens the tall oak door. As soon as we walk through, he wraps his arm around my waist and pulls me close to his side. I know he can feel the anxiety coursing through me and I hate that I've been so miserable around him the past few weeks.

We've been trying for years to have a baby and this is the last and final attempt to make it happen.

I'm tired; no, I'm exhausted from all of the fertility treatments. Between the shots, abstaining from just about everything and the stress that this is my fault I could use some good news.

I've always been a firm believer in the saying that *everything happens for a reason*. I'm beginning to think that there's a reason we were not meant to get pregnant. As much as it kills me inside to think the results may be negative, I'm done trying and putting myself through this heartache.

I've become obsessed with us having a baby and it's taken a toll on my marriage, my social life and I hate the emotional mess I've become.

Keith guides me up to the check-in window and we wait for the receptionist to acknowledge us.

A short female walks toward the giant glass window and slides it open. She has a huge smile forming on her bright red lips as she chomps down on her mouth full of gum.

This is so not how I need to start the day.

"Hiya," she says.

I can feel Keith tense against the side of me and I can guarantee he's just as annoyed as I am.

"Good morning, Emma McIntyre for my nine o'clock appointment with Dr. Chesterfield."

"Ahh yeah, I see your name right here. I'm just here as a temp today and really have no clue what I'm doing."

Keith lets out a grunt and says, "Yeah, we can see that."

"It's fine," I reply.

I move away from Keith just a smidge and reach into my purse to pull out my wallet.

"Here's my insurance card and license. They always take it and make a copy for their records."

The temp continues to chomp down on her gum and reaches for the cards.

With a giggle she says, "Ah yeah, that makes sense. Dorothy is in the back and I'll see what she wants me to do with these. Go ahead and take a seat, I'll be sure to get these back to you before you leave."

"Great, thanks," I say as Keith turns and leads me over to the waiting area.

"Are you fucking kidding me?" Keith asks.

"Just relax, I don't need any added aggravation right now," I tell him as we take our seats.

"You and me both."

For the next few moments we sit in silence as more patients begin to enter the office. My stomach is in knots and I just want to get in there and find out whether we'll be parents or not.

I lean my head back against the wall and close my eyes. Letting out a heavy sigh, Keith grabs onto my hand and intertwines our fingers.

"It'll be okay, Em."

"How do you know it will be okay, Keith? We've been struggling to have a baby for too long. If we're not pregnant this time around, I'm done."

He turns in his chair and faces me. Pulling both my hands into his lap, he looks at me in a way I've never seen before. I'm not quite sure what to say or how to feel right now.

"Emma McIntyre."

I look up and see Dorothy standing in the doorway.

She has the same cheerful look on her face as she always does.

I return a forced smile in her direction and move to stand.

This is it; I'll either leave this office as a mother or a woman that will be changed forever. Either way, life as I now know it will be different.

Keith follows close behind me as we walk through the hallway and into an exam room.

"Mrs. McIntyre, I'll need you to change into this gown and remember the opening faces forward like a robe. I'll be back in a few minutes to check your vitals and then Dr. Chesterfield will be in to see you."

The nurse exits the room, and even though Keith is in here with me, I suddenly feel alone.

Keith pulls the curtain around us so that I'm shielded from the door.

I slowly start to remove my clothes and I watch as Keith takes a seat in the far corner of the room. He's just staring off into space, and as much as I need to know what he's thinking, I don't bother to ask.

After pulling on the gown, I take a seat on the table and pull the white sheet up over my legs. My nerves are causing my stomach to ache and I feel a bit dizzy. The fear of what is about to happen is killing me. *What's going to happen to us if this last in vitro doesn't work? What if we can't make it through this?* The sleepless nights and the stress that has been eating at me has almost become too much to bear. I don't know if I can emotionally pull myself together after hearing the same bad news again.

A knock sounds at the door and I call, "Come in."

The door opens and the curtain is slightly pulled to the side.

"I see you're all set in here. Let's go ahead and get some vitals."

The nurse pulls out a stethoscope and blood pressure cuff. I can only imagine how high the reading will be since I'm a jumbled mess right now.

"Just relax, Mrs. McIntyre. Okay, good, your blood pressure is one seventeen over eighty two, its good. I just need to get your temperature and then I'll need a urine sample."

I nod my head in her direction as she sticks the thermal scan device into my ear.

After my temperature is taken, she tidies up her equipment and places a cup on the counter.

"You can use the restroom in here and leave the sample on the sink."

She gives me a smile and touches my shoulder in a caring gesture. I can guarantee this isn't the easiest job for her, either. The fate of her patients is something she can't control, but she's still trying her best to calm me.

As she moves to exit the room, she pulls the curtain over and I hear the door shut. I look over to Keith and see that he's still staring into the wall.

I grab the cup from the counter and say, "I'll be right back," as I walk to the restroom.

In the restroom I stand for a bit looking into the mirror.

My long dark hair is pulled into a pony tail and a red rim surrounds my hazel eyes. The color of my face is drawn out and I look pale and tired.

Well, it's now or never.

I attempt to remove the lid on the cup, but my hands are trembling. After three times of going through this you'd think I was a pro, but no, I'm still a nervous wreck.

After a bit of a struggle, I'm able to remove the lid and pee in the cup. Before leaving the restroom I seal my fate and wash my hands.

I'm so scared. Not just to find out the results, but not knowing what will happen once my husband and I leave this office.

Walking out of the restroom, I'm met with Keith face to face.

"Are you okay? What's wrong?" I ask.

"Nothing's wrong, Em; I'm just a bit antsy and needed to stand."

"Oh, okay."

I don't like the feeling I'm getting from him. He seems so distant and I don't know what to make of it.

A knocking sound pulls my focus to the door and I call for whomever it is to come in as I climb back onto the table and Keith takes his place against the wall.

Dr. Chesterfield and the nurse both enter and he approaches me to shake my hand.

He's an older gentleman with the heart of a saint, salt and pepper hair and eyes the color of dark chocolate.

"Good morning, Emma, it's so nice to see you again today."

"Morning. Thanks, you too," I reply.

"The purpose of your visit today is to determine if your in vitro was successful. Do you have any questions or concerns for me before we proceed?" He looks between both Keith and I.

I shake my head no. I just want to get this over with and find out whether or not I'm pregnant.

"Why don't we start off with an exam and I'll have Dorothy go ahead with the urine sample."

I watch as the nurse moves toward the restroom for my sample. When she exits with the cup, my heart falls straight to the floor. She's walking away with all the answers I need to know right now. The concern I feel for the next time I'll look into her eyes is eating me alive.

"Mrs. McIntyre, please lie down and place each foot into a stir-up."

I do as he instructs me and just stare up at the ceiling throughout the entire exam. I need Keith here by my side not sitting in the fucking corner. I don't know what he's doing, or hell, even what he's thinking right now.

For the next few moments I lie on the table feeling numb. I understand this is all part of the visit, but I don't know why we couldn't just find out the results first.

"You can go ahead and sit up. I'll leave so that you can get dressed. Dorothy will come back in to get you and bring you into my office. We can discuss the results of the urinalysis and decide on what next steps are best for you and your care."

"Thank you, Dr. Chesterfield, I'll only be a moment."

As the doctor leaves the room, I hop down from the table and quickly change back into my clothes. I really can't wait another minute to find out; it's seriously driving me insane.

I fold up the gown and sheet and place them back on the table.

Without saying a word, I move toward Keith and wrap my arms around his waist.

"I know this is hard on both of us. I need your support now. I need to know that you're in this with me no matter what happens in the next few minutes."

He pulls me into a closer embrace and rests his chin on top of my head.

"Emma, I've been by your side for what feels like forever. No matter what we're about to find out, things will be different. I'm not saying they'll be bad, just different."

A lump forms in my throat and I have no clue how to interpret what he's just said to me.

"Come on, they're waiting on us," he says and takes my hand in his and we leave the exam room.

Dorothy is waiting for us as we walk through the door and leads us to the other end of the hallway and into Dr. Chesterfield's office. He's already sitting behind his desk and stands as we enter the room.

"Thank you, Dorothy. Mr. and Mrs. McIntyre, please take a seat."

My legs begin to tremble as I walk toward the desk. Keith gestures for me to take a seat and he moves to sit next to me.

"I know this is not the type of appointment you look forward to and I want to share the results with you before we discuss anything else."

Dr. Chesterfield's expression is blank; there's no emotion whatsoever.

The lump in my throat is making it difficult for me to swallow and my hands are beginning to sweat.

"I'm sorry, but the test results were negative. I can't begin to imagine your feelings right now, but I want to stress that there are still a variety of options we can discuss."

My body begins to go into panic mode. Even though I knew very well there was a slim chance, it stills hurts so bad to hear the truth.

I look to Keith as tears begin to pool in my eyes.

"Look, Em, I know this sucks and we've been through hell and back. Maybe this is a sign that we should stop trying."

Even though I feel the same way, the pain of hearing those words thrusts a knife into my heart.

Shaking my head I tell both of them, "I won't continue to put myself and my husband through this anymore. We need to come to terms with the fact that we can't have children."

A single tear falls down my cheek and the realization that this may be it for us hits me hard.

Chapter 2

Emma

On the way home from the doctor's office, Keith and I sit in complete silence.

I have an uneasy feeling in the pit of my stomach and I'm not sure if it's from the news that we just received or the fact that I'm not sure what's going to happen between me and my husband.

I watch as the town of Greensboro, North Carolina passes us by and only one thought consumes me. *What happens now?*

Keith and I have been married for the past ten years and during that time we've spent three years trying to have a baby. It's taken an enormous toll on our relationship and after this I don't know how we'll get through the disappointment.

Before all of the fertility treatments and in vitro attempts we were really happy. We've always been that happy go lucky couple that was the life of the party, but now not so much. The two of us have grown apart and at times I feel like we're hanging on by a string. It's gotten so bad, that with my sleepless nights, I've found Keith sleeping in the spare room or on the couch. I honestly can't even remember the last time we were intimate.

I pull my stare from the passing scenery and over to Keith as I hear him clear his throat. Knowing him as well as I do, I recognize that noise; he wants to say something but is trying to keep his thoughts to himself.

"Just tell me what's on your mind Keith."

He looks over at me and then glances back over to the road.

"I don't know what to say right now, Em. I'm just as disappointed as you are, but at the same time I think it's for the best. Ya know?"

"No, I don't know what you mean, Keith. How is this for the best? I thought a baby was something we *both* wanted…right?"

My nerves start to play tricks on me and I'm so worried about what he's about to say next. All this time I thought we were working so hard to become a family and maybe it was never something he wanted at all.

"I'm not in the mood to get into this kind of conversation, Em, can we just drop it?"

I'm appalled by his lack of consideration, I know this is happening to him, too, but he hasn't been the one dealing with the hormonal changes, shots and other shit. I just shake my head and turn toward the window.

"Yeah, because *that* helps make things better," I mumble under my breath.

"Are you fucking kidding me, Em? You know what, just forget it," he says, slamming his hands against the steering wheel.

I jump from his gesture and slide myself closer to the door. Something isn't right and I can't stand the feeling that I have coursing through me.

We pull up into our driveway and Keith stops the truck outside the garage.

"Are you keeping the truck out of the garage for a reason?"

"No, Em, I'm dropping you off and I'm going to go to work. I can't sit here and stare at the walls; I need to get out and get some air. I think we both need to take a breather after the news we got this morning."

"Oh, I see. I was hoping we could spend the rest of the day together."

"Yeah, well I can't read your mind and you didn't say anything. I just need to get away for a few hours to clear my mind. Why don't you call your mom and go for lunch or something."

I don't respond—not that I don't want to—but because I have no clue what kind of words will come out of my mouth if I open it.

Instead of starting an argument, I grab my purse and pull on the door handle.

Keith doesn't say a word, and neither do I, as I hop down out of his truck. I guess he's right--we both need some time to digest the news we just received—it just sucks that we have to do it apart.

I punch in the code for the garage and keep my back turned to him as I hear the truck pull away. I probably should call my parents to let them know the results, but honestly I'd rather be alone. I'll give them a call a little later when the shock wears off a bit.

I toss my purse onto the kitchen table and make my way up to my room. About halfway up the stairs I realize I forgot my phone in my purse. *Shit!* Storming back down the stairs, I grab it and stomp my feet like a two year old back up the stairs.

Lying down on my bed, I close my eyes, hoping that if I take a nap all of this will just be an awful dream.

I fall into a deep sleep thinking about my sweet little baby that I'll never have and the happily ever after I so longed for falling apart right in front of me.

It feels like I only just closed my eyes when I hear my cell phone chirping. Rolling onto my side, I search for the phone.

"Hello?"

"Hey, honey," a sweet and caring voice responds.

"Hi, Mama."

"I didn't hear from you after the appointment and wanted to know how it went."

"Yeah, well, it didn't go so well," I say letting out a heavy sigh.

"I'll be right there," she says and disconnects the line.

Well then, I guess I better get my ass up and out of bed. I toss the cell phone back onto the pillows and make my way toward the bathroom. Even though I was only asleep for an hour or so, I still feel like crap.

I splash some cold water on my face and dry it with a hand towel. Looking up at my reflection, I'm not sure who the woman is staring back at me.

Nothing in my life seems to be going the way it's supposed to anymore.

I know I'll never have a baby.

I know my marriage is about to fall apart.

I know that after today, life will not be the same.

Today has been shit up to this point, but I want to make the most of it now that my mom is coming over. Hopefully, her cheery disposition will help bring me out of this funk.

Looking at my smudged make-up and my messy hair, I quickly pull out my ponytail and attempt to make myself a bit more presentable.

I grab a make-up removal wipe and try to get rid of the black marks under my eyes.

I laugh to myself as I scrub away; the black bags aren't going anywhere.

Just as I toss the wipe in the trashcan, I hear the door open and shut.

"Emma, sweetie, are you down here or upstairs?"

Damn she must have flown over here.

I peak my head out of my bathroom and yell back down to her, "Up here in my bedroom."

The noise of her shoes hitting the hardwood floors echoes through the tall entranceway. I snatch up my mascara and apply a few coats to my long lashes and pout my lips while adding some gloss. I do one more onceover in the mirror before meeting my mom in the bedroom.

Walking into my master bedroom, I see my mom already fixing up my bed.

"Really, Mom, I can do that." I walk over to her and grab the pillow.

"Emma, I was just trying to be helpful."

"I know, Mama, but I can do it. I'm not broken."

She pulls the pillow back from me and sets it down, takes a seat on the bed and pats on the comforter next to her.

Sitting down next to her, she wraps me into her arms. As soon as my chin hits her shoulder the tears begin to fall down my cheeks. My body trembles as I cry into my mom.

Where do I even begin to tell her how I'm feeling right now?

"Shh, my sweet girl, it's okay. I can't make the pain go away, but I can be here for you to lean on me. I'm so sorry this is happening to you."

Through my sobs I listen to the words my mom is using to console me.

The hurt and anger of not having a baby of my own is one thing, but not knowing what is happening between me and Keith is a whole other obstacle.

I pull away slightly from her embrace and wipe away the tears with the sleeve of my shirt.

"There's so much to think about, Mama. It's not just the loss of a baby; Keith and I are growing further apart and I don't know how to put us back together."

"Emma, you are a wonderful, beautiful young woman. Keith is lucky to have you by his side."

"But Mom, he left me. After hearing the worst news ever, he left to go to work."

My mom gives me a puzzled look.

I sniffle, "What?"

"Well, I called your father on the way over here and he was surprised Keith wasn't home with you."

"Why would he be surprised, shouldn't he be with him?"

She shakes her head and confusion overtakes my senses. I back away from her on the bed and attempt to pull myself together.

"Your father said he called and Keith said he needed to take the day off. When your dad asked why, he just said you two needed some time after the news you received this morning."

"I don't understand. He said he was going to work to get out of here. He said he needed a breather. Where the fuck would he have gone? If he's not here or at work…what the fuck, Mom?"

"Emma, there is no need to talk like that."

"Seriously, I'm going through a lot of shit right now. Don't treat me like a child."

"You're right, sweetie. I understand you're upset; just refrain from throwing the f-bomb out at me. I'm still you mother and it's not respectful *or* ladylike."

I stand from the bed and walk toward the center of the room, turn to look at my mom and cover my face with my hands.

"Mom!" I scream. "This isn't the 1950s, *fuck* is an appropriate word to say in any given situation. Please don't start on me about my choice of words right now. I don't need to deal with your lack of approval on top of everything else going through my head."

I watch the look of surprise grace my mother's beautiful face. She gets up to stand and walks toward me. The last thing I want to do is upset her. She's the person I run to when I'm in need; I can't lose that, too.

She wraps her arms around me and pulls me into a hug.

"As much as I dislike the choice of words you're using right now, I'm not here to fight with you. Why don't we go out for a bit and get some lunch. We can talk about everything a bit more, but I think you should get out of this house for a while today."

I nod my head and slowly step away.

"Let me go in the bathroom and wash my face and then we can go."

I turn and walk toward the bathroom. It was just a few moments ago I was doing the same exact routine.

Ugh! I need to get my shit together and pull my emotions back to where they belong. I now know that I'm unable to have the baby I've always dreamed of and I need to be okay with that. As for my husband, I'll deal with him and our issues when we're at home, together. For right now, I want to spend the rest of the day thinking about the things that make me happy—with the one woman that knows me better than anyone—my mama.

Splashing some cool water on my face I reach for the hand towel and dry myself off. I quickly reapply my make-up and add some more gloss to my lips. Looking in the mirror, I know the woman I see is in pain, but for this afternoon, I'll pretend that nothing bothers her and she's happy as can be.

Mom is standing next to the bed watching for me to come out of the bathroom. I walk over to her, pull her into a hug and thank her for always being there for me.

"Now, let's put my shitty life on hold for the afternoon and go have some girl time," I say walking out of the bedroom.

"Sounds wonderful, honey, but do me one favor."

"Sure, Mama, what's that?"

"Smile for me. You're a beautiful girl and I hate to see that pretty face so sad."

I look back and give her the biggest smile I can muster.

"I'll do anything for you, Mama. Come on let's go, I'm starving."

I grab her hand and pull her along my side down the hallway and stairs.

Thank God for this woman right here. If I didn't have her in my life I don't know what I'd do.

Chapter 3

Emma

Mom and I leave the house through the front door and make our way to her fully loaded Audi sitting in the driveway.

My parents have never been ones to flaunt the wealth that they've come into with the contracting business, but Dad insisted that Mom get the car of her dreams.

We hop into her fancy new ride and head down the driveway and out of my subdivision.

I glance at her and an overwhelming feeling takes control of me. Looking at my mom, I see a woman that would do just about anything for her family. In many ways I'd like to think that I'm a lot like her.

Besides her huge heart, she's a beautiful woman. She has the most brilliant blue eyes. For as long as I can remember, she's worn her dark brown hair in a short bob, not a strand out of place. She is the epitome of a perfect, caring and wonderful mom.

I take my eyes off of her and look out the window.

So many thoughts are flying through my mind, and for just one afternoon, I wish I could turn them off. I hate not having control, not knowing what is going to happen next and the fact that—for all I know—the life I've been living is a lie.

I'm pulled out of my self-induced haze when I hear my mom's voice.

"Where would you like to go get something to eat?" she asks, looking at me with a smirk on her face.

I have to be the most indecisive person on the plant and she knows this all too well.

"Mama, I really don't care, you pick," I tell her with a pout on my face.

She giggles and pats the palm of her hand on my leg.

"Okay, Emma, I'll pick this time."

She places her hand back on the wheel and I rest my head back against the passenger's seat, watching as the scenery of Greensboro flies past us.

This is my home, I grew up here.

This is where I started my life; the place I wanted to raise a family.

This is the spot I met my best friend, my husband, and now, I fear that it's the place where we will be torn apart.

Mama's phone begins to chirp from her purse by my feet.

I see my brother, Riley, is calling and I can't help but smile. He's such a fool. We may be ten years apart in age, but I still love him dearly. Growing up, we obviously weren't the closest of siblings, but we totally make up for it now with our daily fighting and bickering.

As I reach down for her purse, she stops me and pushes the hands-free button on her steering wheel.

"Well, good afternoon, honey," Mama says.

"Hey, Mama," he replies, his voice echoing throughout the car.

"Hey, shitbrick!" I shout.

I look over to Mom and she gives me the kindest of her evil glares.

"Well, hot damn! Sweet old Em is with you. Sorry you have to deal with her, Mama."

"Shut the hell up, asswipe," I reply with a giggle.

"Okay, you two; call a truce for a few moments so I can talk to my son in peace."

"Sorry, Mama," we say in unison.

"It's fine. Now, what's up, love?" Mama asks with a huge grin on her petite, yet amazingly beautiful face.

"Dad and I were going to head to Boston's for lunch and he asked me to give you a call. Wanna tag along with us?"

Ha! Of course Riley would pick Boston's as the place to go eat. If there was ever an obsessively die hard Red Sox fan, my brother would win the award hands down.

"Oh, that sounds great; Emma and I were just deciding where we were going to go eat this afternoon."

"No, you mean *you* were deciding. We all know that Em needs help to pick out her shoes for the day," Riley says with a loud laugh.

"Mama!" I screech.

"Seriously, Riley Paul, do I need to slap you?" Mama says, covering her mouth to mask the giggle she lets out.

"Shit, sorry, Mama. It's kinda hard not to make fun of her; it's just too damn easy."

"We'll meet you for lunch on one condition. I don't want a family feud on my hands between you two. You'd think you guys were six and sixteen all over again and I surely don't want to relive those years of torture. I'd rather enjoy the good memories—not the ones of you cutting your sister's hair while she slept."

A loud laugh comes through the speakers and I burst out laughing.

Between the two of us, we sure as hell were a duo that caused both of our parent's grief with our wicked tricks. I agree that sometimes we took things to an extreme, like Riley cutting my hair and me pouring ice cold water in his bed while he slept.

Ahh, such fond childhood memories; some I'd never replace and others I'd like to forget.

If only we could go back to those days—when there wasn't a care in the world. I'd love to move back home and let Mama and Daddy take care of me. Oh wait, I'm a thirty something grown woman…guess that's not in the cards for me anytime soon.

"Mama, I can't make any promises, but I'll try if your daughter can behave."

"Well, thank you, Son. We should be there in about ten minutes."

"Perfect, I'll go grab Dad and we'll meet you there. Bye, Mama, love you."

"To infinity and beyond, my love," she responds.

I have to giggle at my mom's response to my brother. As children, any time one of us would say 'I love you', the immediate response was to infinity and beyond. I love the quirkiness of my family, and to be honest, I'd be lost without them.

My mama has always been there for me—whether it was to take me to dance, gymnastics or cheering practice—she was there. If I needed a shoulder to cry on or celebrate with, she was there. She always seems to know when I need her the most and always comes to my rescue. Mama's the sister I never had and the best friend I'd die without.

I watch as we pull into the mall parking lot and drive toward the restaurant. I can see both Riley and my dad standing on the sidewalk near the front doors. I have to smile at the two men that are such a big part of my life. If there wasn't such an age gap, you'd think they were brothers—both of them stand over six feet tall with brown hair and hazel eyes.

As Mama pulls into a parking spot, the guys come around the car to help us out. I turn to reach for my seat belt and see Riley's smug face plastered against the window.

"Good God, Riley, that face is enough to scare a small child."

He laughs and begins to open the door. I move to step out and he slams the door on me.

"Dude! You could have caught my leg in the door, fucker!" I screech.

He pulls open the door all the way and reaches his hand in to help me out.

"Don't be so dramatic, Em. I was watching where your precious legs were before I shut the door."

"You're lucky, asshat."

Riley helps me out of the car and I glance toward the door to see Mom and Dad waiting for us. They're both standing there, arms crossed and shaking their heads at us.

I see Riley look in their direction and he laughs while saying, "Uh oh."

"We better get a move on before we piss off the 'rents," I whisper, walking up onto the sidewalk.

"Good call, lil lady," Riley says, swinging his arm up around my shoulders.

My brother and I walk up to my parents as Dad is opening the front door. Inside, the restaurant is decked out in just about every piece of Boston paraphernalia you can image. With street signs, pictures, posters and Red Sox memorabilia, it's a haven for a pure fan like my little brother.

His eyes light up, as they always do, like he's a kid that just walked into a candy store.

Riley moves his arm from around me and I walk over to my dad for a hug.

"Hey, love bug," he says squeezing me up against him.

"Hi Daddy, thanks for inviting us for lunch. I really needed this."

"I'm sorry about the news you and Keith got today, but not to worry, everything will be okay."

Oh Daddy, if you only really knew what was going through my mind right now. I wish you could make it all better so that in reality it would be okay.

I pull away from my dad and give him a nod, "I know it will be, thanks to you and Mama."

"Hey, what about me? I'm the best big-little brother in the world," Riley says with a pout on his face

"Please, the only thing you bring into my life is torture," I reply as I look toward him and roll my eyes.

He takes a step toward me and my dad pulls me into him and turns me away from the lethal attack of my baby brother.

The hostess comes to the front stand to greet us and take us to our seats.

"Oh hey, Miss, we may need a children's menu for this little lady right here," Riley says pointing at me.

The hostess gives him a questionable stare.

My dad laughs and tells her to continue what she's doing and that we'd prefer a booth in the back with four adult menus. Mom just shakes her head and slaps Riley across the back.

For the next hour, my family enjoys one another's company while straw wrappers are flying and salt is poured into my water, all courtesy of my loving brother. How he doesn't get us kicked out is beyond me. Maybe it's the fact that he was flirting pretty heavily with the waitress before my dad called him out on it.

After we're all done eating our lunch and two shared desserts, Dad and Riley say they need to get going and prepare for a big contract they're working on out of state. We say our goodbyes with a few hugs, and surprisingly enough, Riley and I walk away without cursing or fighting with one another.

Mom suggests we go do some shopping to keep my mind busy, but I decline knowing very well I should get home and see if my husband has returned.

I'm glad for the distraction of this afternoon, but I also know that once I get home I have a lot to face with Keith.

We begin our journey back to my house and in the pit of my stomach I feel sick. I know it's not because of the lunch I just ate, but because I don't know the first thing I want to say to my husband.

He lied to me saying he was going into work.

Do I confront him and tell him I know he didn't go in or do I let it go just like everything else that bothers us as a couple?

There's so much I should just sit down and talk to him about, but I'm scared. Of what, I don't really know. Will he leave me? Will we fight and make up or will something else happen that I least expect?

I hate this feeling and I just want it to go away.

There's no other option, I have to talk to him about this before it eats me alive.

We pull into my driveway and the garage door is open on Keith's side. He's home.

Chapter 4

Emma

My mom parks her car behind my garage door, shuts off the engine and turns her body to face me.

"Emma, I'll go in with you if you want me to."

I shake my head and will myself to stay calm and not break out into a fit of tears.

Turning to look at her, she has the most sincere look on her face.

"Emma, I don't know what's been going on. This is your life and it's not my place to ask questions or get in the middle of anything. Just know that if you need anything, I mean anything at all, you call us right away."

A single tear falls from my eye and runs down the side of my cheek.

"Mama, I don't know what to do. I don't know if I can fix this."

"I know you're both hurting after today, but you need to talk to him. You can at least do that. If things aren't meant to be then we'll deal with that later. For now, go in and talk to your husband. Communication is essential to making a marriage work and I can tell that right now you're both keeping things inside. Talk to him and call me later if you need me."

I nod my head and lean into my mom for a hug. Pulling away she wipes the tears that are now falling from my eyes.

"Shh, don't cry, sweet girl. I love you."

"To infinity and beyond," I say, wiping my cheeks and checking my reflection in the mirror.

"Call me later, okay?"

"I will, I promise," I say and open the door.

I stand outside the garage watching as my mom backs down my driveway.

Once her car is no longer in sight, I turn and walk into the garage. Before getting to the door, I take a deep breath and turn the knob. Walking through the mud room and into the kitchen I look around, but there's neither sound nor sign of Keith.

Tossing my purse down onto the table, I walk over to the fridge to grab a bottle of water. I shut the door and bam he's standing right there.

"Fuck, Keith, you scared me!" I scream, dropping the bottle of water.

He stumbles backward and I reach down for the bottle.

"Hey baby," he slurs.

"Keith, are you okay?"

I lean in closer to him and notice that he reeks like a bar.

"I'm just fucking great, baby. You don't look happy to see me. Aren't you happy to see me?" he asks, moving in closer to me.

"Have you been drinking?"

"Hey!" he shouts, "I asked you a question first."

"Wait…what? What's going on with you today?"

"Damn you, woman, stop asking so many questions and answer mine. Aren't you happy to see me?" he asks again with a laugh.

He puts his arms around me and pulls me into him.

The sudden contact of our bodies throws my senses off. I can't believe the way I'm feeling right now.

It's been so long since Keith and I were this close, that he's held me and that we've been intimate.

Drunk or not, my body is screaming at me to get closer to him. I let my body fall into him as he starts to nip at my neck. Without even thinking about it, I turn my head to give him better access.

He begins to lick and suck at my ear lobe.

My body begins to react before my brain and I throw my arms around his neck.

"That's my girl; let's move this upstairs so I can have my way with you."

He lets go of me and stumbles backward again.

"Keith, are you sure?"

"Baby, right now I just wanna be with you. Don't worry about anything else, let's just head upstairs."

I nod my head as he grabs for my hand, pulls me through the house and up the stairs.

Once we make it up to our bedroom it's as if he becomes a completely different person than the man that left me earlier.

He looks at me with pure desire in his eyes.

I step in closer to him and he reaches for my waist.

Grabbing for the hem of my shirt, he pulls it up over my head and his cold hands begin to travel from my collar bone slowly down to my hips.

His touch sends chills straight to my core.

I can't believe I'm about to do this, but honestly I don't fucking care. My body has been starved of his touch and I can't wait another second to savor my husband.

I look up at him through my lashes and watch as he licks his lips. He dips his head down and urgently kisses me. His tongue enters my mouth and I can taste the bourbon.

I want him to take me.

I want to get drunk on him.

I want him inside of me…*now*.

He moves his hands from my hips to his jacket.

"Stop," I tell him, "let me."

He nods his head and his hands fall to his side.

I reach out for his fleece jacket and pull down the zipper. It slides off of his shoulders and down his arms and I watch as it falls to the floor.

He's wearing a plain white tee shirt and I take a step back to look at him. I haven't taken the time to see him like this in so long.

His body is firm and toned.

As I reach down for the bottom of his shirt, he steps back to give us some room. I attempt to lift the shirt up over his head, but with his height I can't reach very far.

He lets out a laugh and moves my hands so that he can pull it up and over his head.

My hands instantly move to his chest and my lips find their way to his nipples.

I gently lick one and then the other.

Standing this close to him I can feel his erection begin to grow against my belly.

I let my hands graze over his chest again and lead my way down his stomach, moving closer and closer to the top of his jeans. I unfasten the button and pull down the zipper; all the while my core is aching for his touch.

If I don't get close enough to him I feel as though I might burst.

He kicks off his pants and reaches to remove my jeans. His hand brushes over my panties and the wetness between my legs begins to build.

"Babe," he says.

"Keith, please, just touch me," I beg.

He lifts me and I wrap my legs around his waist.

Walking us back toward our bed, I place my lips against his.

The flavor of the bourbon hits me again and I begin to feel intoxicated by my man.

There's just something about the way he kisses me. His tongue searches out for mine as he lays us down on the bed. He deepens our kiss with his body hovering over mine.

He rubs his erection against me and I let out a moan.

"Keith, *please*," I cry.

"Don't worry, baby, I'm going to make this up to you. I need you as much as you need me. We're going to make things right again."

He rests back on his knees and starts to pull down my panties.

I sit forward and slide his boxer briefs down his legs as far as they can go.

He moves to stand next the bed and kicks them off while reaching behind me to unclasp my bra. In a flash, he comes back onto the bed and props himself over me with his arms.

Bending his head down to me I capture his mouth with mine. I nip at him and lick the crease of his lips until he opens his mouth to allow my tongue to dance with his.

We kiss for what feels like forever and I can barely stand the need I have for my man right now.

I buck my hips up to meet his body, and within a matter of seconds he has me flipped over so that I'm straddling him. I look down and grab his needing erection, moving it toward my warmth and slowly ease down onto him.

"Oh my fucking god," I groan.

"Yeah, baby," he cries out.

I begin to move faster and faster the more our bodies cry out for each other. The movement between us creates such an intense friction, I feel like I'm about to fall over the edge.

"God, this feels so fucking good, baby." Keith moves his hands to my hips and moves me up and down…up and down.

"Mmmhhmmm," I say as I bite down on my lower lip.

He flips me off of him and onto all fours. I know him well enough to know that he's getting close.

"Come here, baby, give me that ass," he says as he smacks me hard.

The vibration pushes me closer to the edge.

He thrusts himself back inside me and reaches his arm around to massage my clit.

It doesn't take long until an orgasm hits me hard. I can feel the waves of pleasure shoot through me from my head to my toes. Throughout my release, Keith continues to pump in and out of me while rubbing my now sensitive area.

"Oh, baby, that's it," he says smacking my ass for the second time.

With the power of his thrusts and the slap on the ass I can feel another moment of ecstasy getting ready to hit its peak.

"Yeah, that's my girl, I can feel you clenching and it's driving me fucking crazy, Em."

He moves his hand from under me and pulls my hips so that my ass is high in the air. He repositions himself so that he's now up on his feet and hitting my core at a totally different angle.

"Holy shit!" I scream as he pulls out and drives himself back into me.

"I know, baby. I won't last much longer so hang on for the ride."

He pounds into me and the angle he's using is creating a feeling that I've never experienced with him before. He's deeper—so much deeper—and it feels so fucking good.

The harder he pushes the more I aim my ass into the air. I can't believe how good this feels, and for a moment, I begin to black out and see spots from the third orgasm he's given me in a matter of minutes.

Keith grabs onto my breast and leans his head onto my back. I can feel the pulsation of his cock inside me and know that he's reached his peak.

His breathing is ragged and I can feel the sweat from his face running down my side.

"Em, I think that was the best sex we've ever had. It was so good that I almost want to wait another few weeks to do it again."

He pulls out of me and rolls off and onto his back.

"Keith, don't even say that. I do have to agree that it was pretty good."

I turn onto my side and rest my head on his chest. Even if it's just for a moment, I want to spend it cuddled into him. I miss this, I miss us.

"I know, baby, things are going to change. I promise."

"I don't want to talk about it right now. I just want to enjoy this moment with you, Keith."

"Okay, babe, close your eyes and let's take a little nap together."

I turn my head just slightly and place a soft kiss onto his chest. This is how I want us to stay; content, at peace and not fighting. We need to be able to get through this together. No matter what, I'm going to try and save my marriage.

Keith runs his fingers up and down my back until I fall fast asleep.

Chapter 5

Emma

I wake to the sound of music—crazy, weird music—and I hear water running.

I roll onto my side and reach out to feel an empty bed.

"Keith!"

I sit up and see that it's almost dark outside but the light from under the bathroom door is on.

Guess Keith decided to take a quick shower, wonder if he'd mind if I joined him.

What am I even thinking?

We haven't had sex in weeks and here I'm thinking about joining him the shower for a quickie. I don't know if it's the pent up frustration or the amazing sex we had a few hours ago, but my libido is ready for round two.

Keith and I were never big on scheduled moments of intimacy, but whenever we could get to one another we'd seize the moment as an opportunity. At least that's how we used to be before the stress of life got in our way.

I step down off the bed and walk toward the bathroom and hear what seems to be rap music.

I listen for a few moments and confirm that it's definitely rap music coming from the other side of the door.

Unless there's someone else in there, Keith has to have lost his mind. He's always been a huge fan of country and rock, but never rap. *Since when does Keith listen to rap?*

I open the door to see Keith standing at the sink, completely naked, shaving his face.

He looks over at me and gives me a questionable smirk.

"Hey babe. Sorry, did I wake you? You were fast asleep when I woke up and I didn't want to disturb you."

I shake my head, "No, you didn't wake me, but your rap music did."

He laughs and looks at me through the mirror while rinsing his razor under the hot water.

"Yeah, about that…this kid was at the bar and started talking about this new guy, Chance the Rapper, so I thought I'd check it out to maybe use when I'm at the gym."

I pull my robe down from the back of the door and laugh at him.

"Whatever works for you, Keith. I just can't think with that music playing in my ears."

"I can think of a few things I can do listening to this music," he says turning toward me, grabbing the robe from my hands and tossing it onto the floor.

My eyes go wide as he picks me up and I instantly wrap my legs around his waist.

"Just think of the movements we can create in the shower listening to these beats," he says with a laugh and wiggles his eyebrows at me.

I laugh at him again as I wrap my arms around him and nuzzle my face into the crook of this neck. I honestly can't stand rap music, but hell, I'll try anything once.

Keith moves us toward the standing shower, opens the glass door and turns on the water. While he waits for the water to warm, I take advantage of the moment and begin to lick, nip and suck along his freshly shaven jaw line and neck. I can feel his erection begin to grow beneath me and a rush of excitement starts to consume me.

To think only a few hours ago I was concerned our marriage was at risk and now we're about to have some hot shower sex. I know that we'll eventually have to talk about what's been going on the past few months, but I don't think anyone would fault me for giving into the desire I feel for my husband right now. And if they did, well tough shit. I'm totally taking advantage of the time with my husband.

Keith reaches his arm back into the shower to feel the water and lifts us into the steaming water while pushing my back up against the cool tile wall. A shiver runs through my body as he captures my mouth with his. He nips at my bottom lip and I open my mouth to invite his tongue to touch mine. I'm lifted just enough so he can position himself beneath me and thrust himself into my warmth. Our bodies rock back and forth as we continue to lock our lips in a passionate kiss.

My hands travel up and down his back and scratch at his skin the closer I come to reaching my climax. He grabs under my ass to lift me higher, pushing himself into me a little deeper.

Together we pant, moan and scream out one another's names as we reach our orgasms together.

Keith lets my body slide down along his until my feet touch the shower floor and I step up on my tiptoes and place a gently kiss to his lips.

"I love you, baby," I say to him, looking up into his grey eyes.

"Ditto, babe," he replies, pushing my hair out of my face.

He turns my body toward the wall and grabs for the shampoo. He lathers his hands with the strawberry scented shampoo and starts to massage the fragrant gel into my long, brown hair. We take turns washing one another for the next few minutes until we're both covered in bubbles. Once we're scrubbed and clean, Keith pulls down the detachable shower head and rinses us both off. I turn off the water and he leans down to me for one more kiss on the lips.

I love this attention he's giving to me right now and don't want this moment to end. I really do miss this side of us; it's been gone for far too long.

We exit the shower and both dry off with our fluffy green towels and head back into the bedroom to get dressed.

As we walk into the room I look over at the alarm clock on the night stand.

"Shit, I can't believe it's already five-thirty."

"Yeah, I know sleepy head. I guess we both needed a nap today."

I look over to him and give him a sly smirk. I open up the top drawer in the tall dresser and pull out a pair of panties and a bra.

Tossing them onto the bed I ask, "Are you hungry? Should I start making us something for dinner?"

"Nah, I need to meet a few of the guys over at the club around seven. We can just grab something to eat there if you want."

I look over in his direction. *Hmmm, was he planning on telling me this or was he just going to head out on his own?*

"Umm...yeah...sure. I didn't know you had plans already. I can stay back here if you're meeting up with the guys," I say walking toward the closet.

I open the door and walk inside, not quite sure what I need to pull out to wear.

He comes up behind me and wraps his arms around my waist.

"Em, I feel like we just took ten steps forward. Don't pull us back to where we started."

I turn to look at him in surprise.

What the fuck is that supposed to mean?

Once again, instead of causing an argument, I just brush it off.

"Okay, okay, I'm sorry."

He tips my chin up to him and kisses me gently on the lips.

"That's my girl. Now let's get dressed and go get something to eat," he says, swatting my ass and moving to his side of the closet.

Sometimes I feel like pushing matters such as this aside only makes things worse. I know this is going to eat at me all night. It really shouldn't, but with how we've been the past few months, I worry about what he thinks and the stuff that goes on in his head.

I close my eyes and take in a deep breath. I need to break myself of these thoughts and get ready to go out for dinner.

Since we're going to the club, I need to dress up a bit, so I pull down a cute black dress from the hanger and a red sweater wrap.

"Hey, babe, which shoes do you think would look better with this dress? Should I go with the wedges or these heels right here?" I ask, pointing to my three inch black stilettos I know he loves.

"Oh fuck, Em, if you wear those shoes with that dress I'll be staring at your legs all night long. I can't promise I won't be dragging you onto the eighteenth hole for a quickie."

I blush at his comment and giggle as I grab up the heels.

"Heels it is," I say, carrying my outfit out of the closet.

I don't know what's gotten into him since this morning. How is it possible for one man to change his whole attitude so quickly? I mean, I'm going along with it, but I'm really about to get whiplash from his change in personality.

We seriously need to sit down and hash all this shit out before I explode one day. Now that the news of the baby is out in the open, I think it's time we start to work on our marriage. The sex today has been amazing, but I know sex alone won't keep us together and happy for long.

Together we get dressed in the bedroom and I can't help but steal a few glances in his direction.

Keith is an attractive man, and when we're happy I can't help but remember all of the good times we've shared in the past ten years. He was my first everything. My first crush in high school, my first and most embarrassing kiss, the first person I gave my heart to and the one and *only* man I've ever made love to. Looking back on those memories, I realize I only want to make that many more with him.

As I step into my dress, I watch as he pulls on his black button up shirt, carefully threading each button into the right hole and tucking it into his grey pants. He's not nearly as tall as my dad and Riley, but he still towers over my five foot two inch frame. He's muscular but not too bulky. I've never been a fan of overly muscular men and the fear that their arms were like a nut cracker waiting to snap my neck off. He has dirty blonde hair that's always trimmed along the sides and bit longer on the top.

He catches me looking at him and he smiles. I continue to watch him as he begins to walk toward me. His grey-blue eyes are striking and one of my favorite qualities of his.

He reaches out for me and pulls me into his embrace.

"Em, you know I love you with everything that I am. We've hit a rough patch over the past few months, but I promise to work harder to be a better husband, you'll see. Big things are about to happen for us. Whether we are able to have a baby or not we'll get through this together and I *will* make you happy."

I nuzzle my head into his chest and breathe in the scent of his after shave, his body wash and fresh clean laundry.

This is the man I fell in love with more than ten years ago and the man I married. I know we have a lot to work through, but if he's willing to try and make this work, then I will too.

I won't walk away from this man—not today, not tomorrow, not ever.

I can only hope that things turn around for us and that we can be happy together again.

Chapter 6

3 weeks later

Thursday February 23, 2012

Emma

The sound of Keith's alarm pulls me out of my sleep. I'm wrapped up in his arms with my head resting on his firm chest. My eyes flutter open and my body moves as he reaches for his cell phone.

I watch as he turns the alarm off and tosses the iPhone onto the bed. Pulling me in closer, he kisses the top of my head.

"Morning, babe," he says.

"Mmmm," I reply.

"Come on, sleepy head, time for us to get up and go for a run."

I shake my head back in forth, tickling his chest with my hair.

"You know how cute you are when you fight me? I'd love to stay wrapped up in you this morning, but we have to get up and hit the streets for at least a good five mile run today."

I look up at him with a pout on my face.

He smiles back down at me and begins to tickle me under my ribs. I burst into a fit of laughter and try to push his hands off of me as he straddles my hips and pins my arms above my head.

"Who's in charge now, Em? We can do this the easy way or the hard way," he says with a serious smirk plastered to his face.

I buck my hips up and try to squirm out from under him.

"No no, little lady. No sex for you until after our run."

He moves and flips me onto my stomach, slapping my ass.

"Let's go," he says, getting off the bed.

I laugh into my pillow and roll onto my back to see he's standing next to our bed in nothing but a black pair of boxer briefs. My eyes travel up his body and I so badly want to stay cuddled up in his arms rather than go for a run on this chilly February morning.

"Fine, fine, I'll get up, but you'll owe me some panty dropping shower sex when we get back."

"Deal!" He shouts moving into the closet.

I giggle while getting out of bed and moving toward my dresser where I grab a sports bra, running pants and top. Even though we're in North Carolina, it's still a bit chilly at six thirty in the morning. God only knows why Keith has to wake up this early on a Saturday to go out for a run.

For the past two weeks, we've been in training mode for an upcoming half marathon we entered in May. I love a good run, but this training is seriously pushing my limits as a recreational runner.

Since the day our fate was determined and we were told we couldn't have a baby of our own, Keith and I have been working on our marriage. We've both put a lot of effort into making some changes, and I have to say, we're really happy again.

When we aren't together, he sends me random text messages letting me know he's thinking of me and when we *are* together he makes sure to touch me and hold me every chance he gets. Spending quality time as a couple is something we've been lacking and having him back in our bed every night has helped me sleep straight through the night….every night.

Our sex life has improved dramatically to the point that we're intimate more now than before we got married. To spice things up a bit, I went to an adult store a few weeks ago and picked up a couple of things to make the bedroom scene a bit more interesting. At first, Keith wasn't into the use of toys, but once he found how much they turned me on and increased *our* orgasms, it's safe to say our sex lives will never be without the use of our toy bin.

I finish getting dressed and make my way downstairs to the garage where Keith is waiting for me.

"We're gonna push ourselves today, Em. No dragging on that last mile. Let's see if we can beat our time from our last five mile and sprint out the last few minutes."

I give him a look of shock and shake my head in disbelief.

He really pushes me to do my best with this whole training thing, but shit, sprinting the last mile is going to *kill* me.

We walk down the driveway and to the stop sign at the end of the block. My techno-pop remix is blasting in my ears and the runner app is set and ready to go. Keith looks back at me and signals for me to start running. We start out with a steady pace for the first mile, and by the time the voice through my ear buds says I've completed mile two, Keith starts to run a little faster.

The cool breeze against my face sends a chill through me as the sweat begins to run down my face.

I follow his pace throughout the first four miles and when mile five comes, the sprint starts.

My legs are burning with each step and I can see our house come into view. I pump my legs faster and faster trying my best to keep up with him. By the time I hit the end of our driveway I feel like I'm about to collapse.

The air coming in and out of my lungs is rough and painful from the cold air.

Keith looks back at me from the top of the driveway and gives me a huge grin. I walk up next to him and bend at the waist putting my hands on my knees.

Air…I need air.

"Damn, babe, you fucking kicked ass," he says, pulling his arm band off and taking his iPhone out of the sleeve.

I continue to steady my breaths as he scrolls through the screens on his phone.

"We averaged a nine minute mile with the last mile clocking in at less than seven minutes."

He reaches his hand out for me and pulls me up against him.

"Breathe, babe, breathe. In through your nose, count one, two, three and exhale through your mouth. You were amazing this morning. I'd say I owe you some fucking hot-ass shower sex."

He tips my chin up to look at him.

"You up for it, or are you too beat from your last mad dash to get to the driveway before me?" he asks with a laugh.

I take in a deep breath through my nose, count and let out a ragged burst of air from between my lips.

"Oh, if it's going to be fucking hot-ass shower sex, then I'm all for it," I reply with a coy smirk.

Keith pulls me in alongside him and wraps his arm around my shoulders as we walk into the garage. He grabs us both a bottle of water out of the fridge and opens one, handing it over to me.

"Small sips, babe, we don't want you cramping for the next Olympic event."

I roll my eyes and smile up at him while taking in a small sip.

My phone begins to ring from my arm band and I hand my bottle of water over to Keith while wrestling my phone off my arm.

I see my mom's name on the display and can't imagine why she'd be calling me so early on a Saturday morning.

"Hey, Mama."

"Hi, sweetie," she replies, "your father and I are heading out of town for the day and I just wanted to let you know. We have a few things we need to get done in Raleigh and I didn't want you to worry if you called and neither of us was around."

"Oh, okay, well thanks for the heads up. Keith and I just finished a record breaking five mile run and I'm about to go upstairs for a shower. Is there anything I can do to help?'

"No, we should be home later this afternoon. I'll give you a call when we get home. Maybe we can meet over at the club for a late dinner. Give your brother a call and tell him to be on standby," she says with a laugh.

"Ok, Mama, enjoy your trip and be safe. Tell Dad I love him and we'll see you guys later tonight."

"Will do, sweet girl. I love you."

"To infinity and beyond," I reply.

The call disconnects and I smile over at Keith as he shakes his head at my family's silliness.

"Is everything okay?" he asks.

"Yep, Mom and Dad are just heading to Raleigh for the day to run some errands. They'll be back later this afternoon and thought we could all go to the club for dinner."

"Sounds good to me. I have a bit of work I need to do for your dad at the office this afternoon, but it shouldn't take too long. When I'm done we can get ready and meet them over there."

He reaches his arm out for me to come into his side and I lean my head against his chest.

"Thank you so much for making the past few weeks as amazing as they've been. I'm so glad we've been able to move past some of the toughest times and be happy again."

"Me too, babe," he says. "Now, let's get you upstairs and naked."

Together Keith and I walk into our home and make our way up to our bedroom. For the next thirty minutes we have amazing shower sex and I help him get dressed for his afternoon at the office.

I run a few errands of my own around town and start to clean up the house when I hear my phone ringing in the other room. I set down the basket of wash and head into the kitchen to grab my phone.

Shit, I missed Riley's call.

I toss the phone into the wash basket and carry the piles of clean clothes up to my bedroom. The phone starts to ring as I'm walking up the stairs, but since my hands are full I can't grab for it.

Once in the bedroom, I set the basket down on the bed and reach for my phone. It starts to ring again and I see my brother's name on the display screen.

I swipe my finger across the screen and answer his call.

"Damn it, Riley, my hands were full and I couldn't answer. What the hell is so urgent that you had to call me three times in less than a minute?"

His breathing is quick.

"Em, where are you?" he asks, his voice is broken and he sounds upset.

"I'm at home cleaning and doing wash. Why, what's up? Are you okay? You sound upset." "Is Keith there with you, Em?"

"No, he's at the office doing some work for Dad. Riley, what's going on and why are you asking stupid questions?"

"Em, I need you to get over to General Pines Hospital. I'm on my way over there right now."

"Riley, what the fuck is going on and why do we both need to get to General?" I ask with panic in my voice.

"Em, please just get your fucking ass over there! There's been an accident and Mom and Dad were just rushed there by Medicopter."

My body goes numb and I drop the phone to the floor. For a split second my entire world begins to spin and I'm all alone.

I bend down and pick up the phone that's now lying by my feet.

"Em, you there?"

"Sorry, umm yeah, I'm here. I'll be there if fifteen minutes," I say as tears begin to pool in my eyes.

"Drive careful, Em. I should be at General in five minutes. Meet me outside the ER doors."

"Okay, Riley, and please tell me they'll be okay."

Chapter 7

Emma

I rush down the stairs, grab for my purse and toss my cell phone into my pocket as I make my way out into the garage. My hands are shaking as I push the start button in my car.

Slowly, I try to regain my composure as I attempt to back out of my garage and down the long windy driveway without running into anything. A million things are running through my head as I drive over to General Pines Hospital.

I just spoke to Mama this morning. She sounded happy and excited to see us all for dinner tonight. This can't be happening.

A loud ringing sound triggers my attention and I see Keith's name appear on the car's navigation screen. I push the hands-free button on the steering wheel and answer his call.

"Hello?" I answer in between sobs.

"Em, baby, are you okay? Riley just called, and I'm on my way, but it may take me a bit longer to get there coming from the office."

"Keith, I need you there with me!" I cry out.

I hear him let out a breath of air.

"I know, Em, I'll get there as soon as I can. Riley's there now and will meet you right outside the ER. Drive safe, baby, and just know that I love you."

"I love you, too."

The line disconnects and I watch the town of Greensboro pass me by as I fly through the streets.

I need to be there; I have to give them the strength and support to be okay.

Oh God, if anything were to happen to my parents I don't know what I'd do.

Pulling into the medical complex of General Pines, I navigate myself with each sign leading me to the ER entrance. I pull up to the emergency room parking lot where I can see Riley standing outside waiting for me as I pull into an empty front row spot. He comes running over to my car and opens the door.

"Riley, what do you know?" I ask, stepping out of my car.

"I don't know much of anything yet. I received a call about an hour ago saying they were in an accident and were being flown here by the Medicopter. You were the next call I made. When I got here I checked in with the triage nurse, but they hadn't gotten here yet. Actually, they should be landing any moment. Let's get inside and see if the nurses have any updates to share with us."

I nod my head and lean into my little brother. Thank God I have him here with me right now; I need all the strength and support I can get until I hear both my parents are going to be okay.

Together we walk through the automatic entry doors of the ER. The smell of the hospital hits my senses as soon as we walk in and my eyes immediately go to a doctor walking toward us.

"Hi, are you Riley Kincaid?" He asks extending his hand. "I'm Dr. Patrone."

"Yes, I'm Riley Kincaid and this is my sister Emma McIntyre. Have our parents arrived yet?" Riley asks the doctor.

"The Medicopter is due to land any minute, but I wanted to come down and find you before they arrived. You are more than welcome to come up to the trauma center and wait in the visitors lounge until we know more about your parents' wellbeing."

"Excuse me, Dr. Patrone, is there anything you can tell us about our parents. Are they okay, will they be okay?" I ask as the panic begins to take over my emotions.

"I'm sorry, Mrs. McIntyre, but I don't have anything reassuring to share at this time. Once they arrive and we get them into surgery we'll be able to determine the severity of their injuries."

"Surgery!" I scream.

Riley pulls me in tighter against him and I begin to sob into his shirt.

"Shh, Em, let's just head upstairs with the doctor and wait to see what they can tell us once Mom and Dad get here."

I pull away from my brother and look into his hazel eyes filled with tears. I nod and follow the doctor through the ER and toward the elevator.

The silence between us is driving me mad as we make our way up to the sixth floor.

Riley grabs onto my hand and escorts me off the elevator and into a white-walled hallway, leading us to the waiting area. The doctor turns to face us and shakes both of our hands.

"As soon as I know anything I'll come out or send a nurse to speak with you two."

"Thank you, Dr. Patrone, we'll be fine out here. Just take care of our parents," Riley says.

The doctor exits the waiting area and I begin to pace in the empty room. I look over to my brother and see that he's taken a seat in one of the chairs.

"Come on over and sit down. You're driving me nuts walking around like that."

"Riley, I'm a nervous wreck. I can't sit down right now. I wish Keith was here with us. I need him to be here with me."

"I know, Em, but right now there's nothing any of us can do."

Ugh, I hate not having control over moments like this. No matter how many prayers I chant in my head, my parents' health is at stake and there's nothing I can do about it.

For the next few moments I continue to pace and stare out the window facing the parking lot.

I hear the automatic doors open and see a team of white coats approaching me and my brother.

I walk toward the entrance of the lounge and Riley comes to my side.

"Mr. Kincaid, Mrs. McIntyre. I'm Doctor Phillips, Chief of the Trauma Unit at General Pines. I hate to meet you both under these circumstances, but I have news regarding your parents. Please, have a seat," he says, motioning to the chairs behind us along the wall.

Riley grabs onto my hand and leads me to a seat.

"Your parents were part of an eight car pile-up involving a tractor trailer on highway 40. The medics had to use the Jaws of Life to remove them from the vehicle and they were immediately flow to our hospital for care. Our team of surgeons was on standby awaiting their arrival due to the severity of their injuries."

The doctor stops for a moment and I can feel the blood draining from my face. Even though he hasn't told us the news, I feel a stabbing pain in my chest. Riley wraps his arm around my shoulders and I begin to sob uncontrollably.

"I'm so sorry to tell you that before the Medicopter landed, both of your parents passed away in flight. The injuries they sustained impacted their spinal columns and their internal organs, causing them to bleed internally. There was nothing the doctors on the copter could do to save them. I know how painful this may be to hear, but I can assure you that they passed away without any pain. They were unconscious when the medics arrived at the scene. I'm so sorry for your loss. If you'd like to come back to the OR and see them, the nurses will escort you back in a few minutes."

I turn into my brother's body and let my emotions take over. This has to be a dream—it can't be happening to us. Our parents were two of the most caring, loving and supportive people in the world. Why would they be taken away from us like this?

Riley's body begins to shake and I can feel the tears he's trying so desperately to hold in. I know he's only trying to be strong for me, but he needs to grieve as well.

"We'll give you two a few moments to yourselves and a nurse will be out to get you momentarily. Again, I'm so sorry for the pain you must be feeling."

I watch as the team of doctors leaves the room and my head falls onto my brother's arm.

My heart begins to ache and the pain flowing through my veins is unbearable.

"Riley," I say pulling away from my brother and looking up into his eyes, "I can't believe this is happening. I just spoke to Mama this morning, and if I'd have known this was going to happen I would have told them to stay home. I should have told her to stay home," I cry.

"Em, nothing you could have said or done would have prevented this from happening. As much as I hate to say this, even the stupidest, most painful fucking things happen for a reason. I know the news we just heard is unbearable right now, but we need to lean on each other. I can't take it away or make it better for you, but I *will* be here for you to mourn, grieve and remember every memory we've shared with them. I can't even *begin* to think about anything else right now. I want them to be here so badly, but they're not, and we need to remember them…everything about them together."

I hear the words coming out of my brother's mouth, but honestly, it's not sinking in. I can't believe this is happening. I just wish it was all a bad dream and Keith's alarm is going to go off and wake us up.

I close my eyes and rest my head on my brother's shoulder as I continue to cry for the loss of my parents—my dad, my mom and my best friends. Through closed eyes I can picture every moment I've shared with them since I was a small girl. Just about every memory I have with them was happy. Together, they were a dynamic duo wanting to bring happiness to just about every person they met.

My father had the most caring demeanor. No one would ever have a hurtful thing to say about him. Ugh, it hurts so bad to know that they're gone. Riley and Dad were doing so well with the business and I was beyond proud at how far they'd come in such a short amount of time. They were going to take over the east coast with RPK Contracting. How will we as a family, or the business, ever be the same without them? My mama was the sweetest woman in the world. I looked up to her for so many things. She was always there for us no matter how silly, dumb or crazy we made her. She was proud of her family and did everything she could to keep us close.

Riley pulls me in tighter against him as the tears cascade down my cheeks. I open my eyes to the sound of the elevator doors opening.

Keith comes running into the waiting area and I jump to my feet rushing toward him.

"Have you guys heard anything?" he asks.

I nod my head into his chest while the tears fall and my sobs become louder.

"Oh babe, tell me. What did the doctors say?" he asks in a soft tone, rubbing his hands up and down my back.

"They're gone, Keith. Mom and Dad are gone, we've lost them forever."

Keith moves us over to the chairs and I fall into his lap. I sit with him like this for a few moments until the nurse comes in to take us into see our parents.

"I don't know if I can do this," I tell Riley and Keith.

"Yes you can, Em. We need to do this together and we will. You have both of us here to help and support you."

I grab onto the hands of my brother and my husband and move into the trauma rooms to say our goodbyes to our mom and dad.

Chapter 8
One week later
Thursday March 1, 2012

Emma

Sitting down at the kitchen table, I sip on a mug of coffee. I turn my head to look out the window and see that the sunshine is starting to pull through the clouds.

A smile creeps across my face, and for a moment I feel hopeful. It's the first time I've felt like this in a few days.

The pain of losing my parents is still a constant ache in my heart. Every day I wake up hoping to hear my mom's voice one more time or have my dad pull me into his arms.

I miss them so much.

Yesterday was one of the hardest days of my life as we laid them to rest in our family's cemetery plot. Riley and Keith were a huge help getting all of the arrangements in order, but the whole planning thing took a lot out of me. There were times I would break down into full sobs in front of a distant family member or the funeral director, but Keith kept reminding me that it was all part of the healing process and everyone understood what I was going through.

Today is going to be even more of a mess; at least it will be in my opinion.

We have an appointment with my parents' lawyer for the reading of their will. The last thing I want to deal with is who gets what, but at the same time there are so many finances that we have to go through and get in order before the phone calls start coming our way. Keith and Riley have been dealing with the business end of things and I know we have to decide what to do with the house and a few of their other properties and possessions.

I haven't stepped foot in their house or RPK Contracting since the accident. I just can't get myself to do it.

I hear Keith's footsteps coming down the stairs and feel his hands running up and down my back.

"Hey, babe," he says in a cheery tone.

I almost want to blurt out, 'why the fuck are you so happy?', but I know it's not appropriate and the wrong thing to do.

"Hey," I respond.

I watch as he pulls out the chair next to me and sits down. He turns my chair to face him and brings my hand in his. Looking at me with his grey eyes and a smile on his face, I can't help but give him a half smile in return.

"Do you remember when I told you that big things were going to happen for us, babe?"

I shrug my shoulders, not really giving a shit what the hell he's talking about.

"Come on, Em, I told you a few weeks ago that I was working with some guys at the club, remember?"

"I'm sorry, Keith, but I really don't remember. There's just a lot on my mind right now. Besides, how do you have time to work on a project with the guys when you and Riley have your hands full with RPK Contracting?"

"Don't worry about that. Something huge just fell into my lap and it's going to make our lives so much better, you'll see."

"Okay, Keith, if you say so, but for now we need to get going. Riley is meeting us at the attorney's office and I honestly just want to go and get this over with. Dealing with Mom and Dad's estate is not something on my list of favorite things to do."

He leans forward and kisses me on the forehead.

"Don't worry, babe, things are about to change, and I promise you everything will be taken care of and we'll be in good hands."

He gets up from his chair and scoots it in under the table.

"Oh, by the way, once all of this is squared away today, I think you and I should think about what role Riley will be taking on in the business. Honestly, he's still really young to be leading a business like RPK Contracting. He's made a few pretty big errors in the past few weeks and I don't want to jeopardize the reputation of your father's business to a kid."

Oh my God, he's acting like such a douche bag.

"Keith McIntyre, how dare you suggest that Riley would do anything to hurt my father's business? The two of them worked their asses off to make that place what it is today," I reply with a tone of disappointment.

I watch as Keith turns around with a scowl on his face.

"Em, this is not the time to be having this argument. All I was saying is that we don't want a young kid like him with no experience in the business world running things. Your father established a reputable business, we can't jeopardize that. I'm just trying to look out for RPK and allow it to grow like your dad would have wanted."

I look over to him and nod my head, "I guess you're right. I love my brother and I know he'd never do anything to intentionally hurt the business, but perhaps we need to look into some other options. Let's just go to the will reading and we can take things from there, okay?"

"Sounds good, baby, let's go."

I get up from the table and place my mug in the dishwasher. Keith is already standing at the door with my purse and phone in his hands. I understand that this isn't a hug loss to him, they weren't his parents after all, but he really could tone down his level of excitement. We're going to my parents' will reading, not a party.

I follow Keith out the door and into his truck. He opens the passenger's side door for me and I grab onto the handle and step onto the running board to get in. He shuts the door as I fasten my seat belt and wait for him to get in.

As we pull down the driveway I close my eyes and rest my head back on the smooth leather seat.

I don't know how much more energy I have, let alone if I even have the strength to get through another day.

Keith reaches for my hand and intertwines our fingers.

"I got you, babe, I promise. I told you we'd be okay and I'm keeping my word. One more day of going through this stuff and you won't have to worry about any of it ever again."

He looks over at me and smiles.

I don't understand him. How can he be so sure of himself and act like the pain I have will go away? I lost my fucking parents for Christ's sake and he acts like I just got my wisdom teeth pulled out.

I don't have it in me to argue right now; I can't even muster an emotion or something to say in response to him. I just want to get to the attorney's office and see my brother. Riley understands how I feel and what I'm going through right now. Keith on the other hand, well, I have no clue what the hell he's thinking.

We pull into the office complex and I spot Riley's Durango as soon as we pull into our spot. I don't even wait for Keith to come around and let me out. I open the door, hop down onto the pavement and rush to my brother.

Riley pulls me to him and squeezes me into a hug.

"Em, what's wrong? Are you crying?" he asks.

He tries to pull me away to look at me, but I won't budge.

"What happened?" he asks.

"I don't know. She was fine on the way over here," Keith interjects.

I pull away from my brother and glare at my husband.

"No, I *wasn't* fine on the way over here, Keith. I've been a mess for the past week, but you continue to brush my parents' death under the rug like it's nothing. You have no idea how I feel or what it's like to lose a parent. I miss them more today than the day I found out they were dead. I'm not okay today and I won't be for a very long time. I'd rather have my mom and dad here with me than anyone else."

My emotions take over me and I fall to the pavement in a fit of tears. Riley immediately bends down to me and pulls me back up alongside of him. He wraps his arm under my arms so that I can't collapse to the ground again.

"Em, I know this sucks right now, believe me I feel it, too. We have to get through this stuff together so that we can move forward with the things that were most important to Mom and Dad. I miss them, too, and I know they'd want us to be strong. Can you be strong for me, for them?"

I tilt my head up to look into his hazel eyes. I know he's hurting just as much as me, if not more. He'd been Dad's partner in crime since he was a little kid. It's as if our second half was taken away from us and we have this huge empty spot to fill. No one can understand the pain we feel like we do.

I nod my head and wipe away my tears with the sleeve of my shirt. I look over to Keith and see that he's standing watching us with a look of hurt on his face. I walk over to him and put my arms around his waist.

"I'm so sorry, Keith. I didn't mean to yell at you or take my hurt out on you. I'm emotionally unstable right now and I don't know how to get through a time like this without her. I understand that they're not coming back to us, but it just hurts so damn much."

He pulls me in tighter against his chest and squeezes my back.

"I know, Em, and I'm sorry for being so inconsiderate of your feelings. I didn't realize you were still hurting so badly."

He leans down to kiss my forehead and I pull away to look up at him.

"Let's just go inside and see what Mom and Dad's fate has left us to work with. If nothing else, we'll get the answers we need to handle the estate."

"That's my girl, come on."

Keith and I follow Riley into the professional building and take the elevator up to the fourth floor. We walk into the attorney's office and let his receptionist know we're here for the Kincaid Will reading.

I take these few moments to gather my thoughts and pull my emotions into check. I need to deal with this better than I have all the others things we've done. As much as I hate that they're gone, I need to move past the grieving process and get back to my life.

With or without them, my life must go on.

I look up to see a tall man in a suit walking toward us; there's no way this guy could be my parent's attorney. He looks like he's younger than Riley.

"Good morning, sorry to meet under these circumstances, I'm Jax Bryant. I've been working with your parents for the past few years."

My brother extends his hand and introduces us to Mr. Bryant as we all shake hands.

"Ah, Keith, nice to finally meet you. Thank you so much for getting me the copy of the will. Mr. Kincaid was always so persistent about only having one copy and that he'd be the one to hold onto it for safe keeping."

"No trouble at all, I knew right where he kept it and was glad I could be of some assistance during this time."

I look over at Keith and smile. I had no idea he'd been asked to keep an eye on my parent's will. I'm not quite sure why they wouldn't have asked me or Riley, but I'm sure it's because they didn't want to burden either of us with a will in the event they were to pass away suddenly.

Chapter 9

Emma

The four of us walk into Mr. Bryant's office. Immediately my eyes scan the room. The look of his office is quite professional and elegant.

The walls are painted in a light beige color and he has the room decorated with dark wooden furniture. I notice a leather couch and loveseat off to the side and a few bookcases filled with legal journals and books. The wall behind his desk is covered with various degrees and military memorabilia.

For a young looking guy, his office is quite impressive.

"Please, take a seat and we can get started," he says.

Keith, Riley and I take a seat over on the leather couch as Mr. Bryant sits on the loveseat with a file folder in his hands.

I can't get over this guy.

He's an attractive younger man with dark hair and even darker eyes. He's wearing a navy suit with a crisp white shirt and striped light blue and navy blue tie.

"Do you have any questions for me before we begin?" he asks, looking between the three of us.

I shake my head and look over at Riley who shakes his head as well.

"Okay, well to start, the date of this will is quite a few years ago. Riley, I believe you were still in college at the time your parents drew up this document with my father. I will summarize the key elements of the will for you and then the two of you are more than welcome to read its entirety and ask any questions you may have for me."

He seems very business minded and not one to start small talk.

"Yes, that's fine with us, thank you," I reply.

"Emma McIntyre, you've been elected as the executor of the will and have sole power attorney over your parents' estate, possessions and any other property to which they were entitled. You are granted permission to share such items or the wealth of such items with your sibling, Riley Kincaid."

Mr. Bryant takes a breath and looks to the two of us as I grab onto my brother's hand for moral support.

"There is one possession of your parents that does not include you, Riley. Per your parents' last will and testament, the business of RPK Contracting is to be given dual ownership to your older sister Emma McIntyre and her spouse Keith McIntyre."

I hear Riley take in a deep breath and his fingers begin to clench mine.

Ouch. I pull away from the pain of my now broken fingers.

"I'm sorry, Em, I didn't mean to hurt you," he whispers.

"I know, Riley, we'll figure this out, okay?"

He nods his head and gives me a forced smile.

"Here is a list of items, properties and portions of their financial estate. You will need a death certificate to claim these, especially the life insurance policy and any other financial investments that they had prior to their death."

Mr. Bryant looks to both Riley and me and I nod my head in understanding.

"I know this is a lot to take in and I'm certain the funeral director has ordered you enough death certificates. If for some reason you need additional ones, let my receptionist know and she'll be more than happy to assist you."

"Okay, thank you," I respond.

Mr. Bryant nods his head and hands both Riley and me a copy of the will.

"I'd prefer if you took the time to review this document while you're both here. That way you can ask questions and I can have you both sign that you witnessed the reading and acknowledged your acceptance of the will."

Riley seems to be at a loss for words so once again I choose to speak up, "That's fine with us."

For the next few minutes, Riley and I peruse the will, well, at least *I* do. Each time I look up at my brother it seems as though he's staring off into space. I finish reading through the handful of papers and neatly stack them on the table in front of me.

"Actually, I do have a question Mr. Bryant."

"Yes, Emma, what is it?" he asks while sitting back down on the love seat.

"What if Riley wished to partner with Keith and I in all endeavors related to RPK Contracting? I mean, it's really his business with my father and I can't believe my parents would have chosen to keep him away from it."

"Well, as I said earlier, this will was dated a few years ago. I'm not too sure what your parents' intentions were then or prior to their death. If Riley chooses or wishes to be a part of RPK Contracting, that is a deal that you and your spouse will need to work through with him. If ownership is the case, then you are more than welcome to use my legal counsel at your disposal. I was quite fond of your parents and if there's anything I can do to be of any assistance, please let me know."

Keith nudges me in the side and look over at him. He gives me a questionable glare and I scrunch my brows at him. *What the hell is his problem?* I direct my sights back to Mr. Bryant.

 "We'll get this figured out and be in touch with you as soon as possible."

"Thank you, Emma. Are there any other questions at this time?"

I look over to Riley and see that he's still zoned out, looking through the office windows.

"I don't believe so; if anything comes up we'll be sure to contact you."

"I'll need you both to sign the original document and I have copies of everything here for you in these envelopes."

I take the pen from him and sign my name then hand the pen over to my brother.

"Thank you so much for your time today. I am truly sorry for your loss; your parents were good people."

I give Mr. Bryant a smile and thank him for his time.

The four of us stand and he escorts us out of his office and back to the waiting area.

"Patty, if Riley or Emma need anything I advised them to contact us."

Patty smiles at us and nods her head.

Together we walk out of the building and out to the parking lot. Riley walks directly to his SUV and gets in, leaving us without a word.

"Well, *that* was unexpected," Keith says.

"I don't understand what just happened. RPK Contracting was Daddy and Riley's dream; why would they take it away from him?"

"Maybe your parents knew more about him then they let on. Like I told you earlier, he's been making some major errors on the jobs and his last bid was way under price. We're going to wind up taking a huge cut on the job because of his lack of accuracy."

"It doesn't make any sense to me; it's not like him. This is his *life*; it was his dream to run the business with Daddy."

"Em, don't worry yourself over it now. Let's get you home so you can relax for the rest of the day. I have to get back to the office and finish up some paperwork for jobs we have lined up these next few weeks. It's going to get a bit hectic over the next few months until the crews get used to your dad not being around. I need to step in, and quickly, before things get out of hand."

"I agree, we can't let the business fall apart without Daddy."

He wraps his arms around me and holds me tightly against him.

"Okay, babe, let's get you home."

Keith opens the passenger's side door for me and I hop on into the cab of the truck.

He's right—we need to act on things now before it's too late. I just don't know what's up with my little brother. I guess I'll give him some time to digest the news and call him later today. If he needs me before then he knows how to reach me. I have enough on my plate than to worry about him. It'll just piss him off that much more.

Keith drives us back to our house and drops me off before heading back to the office.

Once at home, I pace around the rooms trying to find something to take my mind off of our latest news.

The house is clean, the laundry is done, shit, what the hell am I going to do?

I look over at the key rack hanging in the kitchen. I see Mom and Dad's key gleaming at me as the sunlight hits the metal on the key ring.

Well, if this isn't a sign then I don't know what the hell is anymore.

I grab my purse, cell phone and the key ring off the hook. Here goes nothing. Time to head over to the house and see how it feels to be in there without them.

On the ride over to their house, years of memories flash through my mind. Birthdays, holidays and weekend dinners are some of the fondest thoughts I have of my parents. My mom's smile always lit up a room and the banter amongst my brother and I would drive them both nuts. But no matter what we did they were always still there to support and comfort us when we were in need.

I pull into their subdivision. They built this house shortly after Riley was born. This is the place that I called home before I went off to college. As I round the corner their house comes into view and I can see the back of an SUV parked in the driveway.

As I get closer, I see that it's Riley's Durango parked behind Dad's garage door. I pull up into the driveway and park on Mom's side.

Getting out the car, I look around the yard to see if he's outside. Not catching sight of him, I walk up to the front door, turn the handle and open it.

"Riley," I call.

I hear no response.

I walk around the first floor, but can't seem to find him. I begin to make my way up the stairs when I hear sobbing coming from one of the bedrooms.

"Riley," I call out again.

At the top of the stairs I see his old bedroom door shut.

What a punk.

I walk to his door and turn the knob. Opening the door, I see him sitting on his old bed. I take the few steps needed to stand in front of him and pull him into a hug.

"How did you know I'd be here?" he asks while crying.

I've rarely ever seen my little brother cry. Even at the funeral he was strong and supportive of his big sister.

"I didn't. I was at home with nothing to do and found myself driving over here. It's the first time I've been in their house since they've been gone."

"Em, why? I don't get it. Why would they take me away from the business? That place was all I had. Dad was teaching me everything he knew so that I could run it with him one day."

"I honestly don't know, Riley, but if it's something you want then we'll work together to make it happen."

He shakes his head and it falls between his knees.

"Em, I just don't know anymore. So much has changed over there in the short time since Dad's been gone. It's only been a week and already I'm getting pushed back from my crew and my jobs."

"Look, Riley, I can't get between you and Keith on this. That's something you need to work through with him. I can't be put in the middle."

"Yeah, I know. I'm sorry for saying anything."

For the rest of the afternoon my brother and I sit in our parents' home. Riley was right—so much as happened in such a short amount of time and a lot of decisions need to be made.

I just really don't know where to start.

Chapter 10

Five Months Later

Friday August 3, 2012

Emma

Lying upstairs in my bed, I listen to the rain as it beats against my bedroom window. I've opened and closed my eyes about a hundred times already this morning. I just can't seem to pull myself out of my cozy slumber.

It's supposed to be another hot and gloomy day in the town of Greensboro and I really don't feel like getting out of bed. I'm supposed to meet Riley for lunch in a few hours and I know I should get my ass up and moving…I just don't want to quite yet.

Every day seems to be more bearable than the one before.

It's been a little over five months since my parents' tragic death, and even though I miss them like crazy, we've all seemed to move on and start living our day to day lives again.

Keith is at work from dawn until midnight taking care of the business at RPK Contracting and Riley…well, Riley has sort of pushed himself away from all of us. I'm not sure what he's been up to, but the distance between us has grown drastically since the day we ran into one another at Mom and Dad's house. I pretty much had to beg my brother to meet with me today for lunch. By the way Keith talks, all Riley has been doing is screwing up one contract after another.

It was tough on us both having to go through our parents' things and sell the house, but neither of us wanted to live there on our own. The memories in that house alone were enough for me to fall apart and cry. Every corner I took—each room we'd walk through—reminded me of them. There was just no way I could keep that house.

It didn't take long to sell once it was put on the market, but the day the new owners met to sign the papers was a day that hurt like no other. It was like the last ounce of closure we needed to say our final goodbyes to the place we once called home for so many years.

I still go visit Mom and Dad every week at the cemetery. I talk to them for hours, but it's still not nearly the same as looking them in the eyes and having their arms wrapped around me.

There are still a lot of other aspects of the estate I need to deal with, but honestly I'm in no rush to manage their financials and other possessions. At some point I know I need to get into Dad's office and go through his paperwork. If only I can get in there long enough without Keith telling me to get out. I've tried to become a part of the business, but the more I show up at RPK Contracting the more I'm pushed away by my husband. I honestly don't know what's going on over there, but Keith seems to have taken charge and assures me that everything is running smoothly.

The hours he's been putting in on the job, plus this project he's been working on with the guys from the club, has pushed us away from one another all over again. Almost every night I eat dinner alone and by the time he gets home from work I'm already asleep in our bed.

As much as I want us to go back to where we were five months ago, I don't know if it's possible. We've had a few events and social functions I've attended with him, but I felt more like a guest of his than his wife. We rarely talk, let alone find moments to be intimate. I've come to hate the monotonous pattern that has become our lives. He's distant in more ways than one and I get the sneaky suspicion he's been hiding something from me. I'd rather not argue with him in the short time we *are* together, so once again I'm stuck pushing our troubles and uncertainties under the rug.

I wish my mom was here to talk to, lean on and help me get through these marital troubles. I know Dad worked long hours and had to be away for travel every now and then, but they still managed to keep their love for one another strong.

What a hot mess we are. I wish I had the ability to look into a crystal ball and know where we'd be in five years. Maybe then I'd have the peace of mind to move on and forget about the small shit we deal with on a daily basis.

Letting out a heavy sigh, I glance at the clock on Keith's nightstand. *Ugh, it's already ten o'clock.* I need to get my butt in gear and hop in the shower.

I toss the sheet off my body and swing my legs off the bed. Rubbing my sleepy eyes, I make my way toward the bathroom.

An hour should be plenty of time to get ready, but I honestly have no motivation to do anything today.

I turn on the shower jets and strip myself of my tee-shirt and panties. I pull down two fluffy green towels from the rack and hang them on the hook next to the shower. Reaching my hand in to the shower to test the water and feeling it's just right, I get in and let the warm water hit me in the face. I pour a small dap of strawberry scented shampoo into the palm of my hand and my senses come to life. After washing my hair, I shave my legs and soap up my body with my body wash. It's amazing how much more awake I feel after a good shower.

I get out and dry myself off from head to toe. Pulling my hair out of the towel, I look in the mirror. My hazel eyes are trimmed in red and the bags under my eyes are bigger than they were yesterday. The stress of the past few months is seriously getting to me. There has to be a way to relieve myself of some burdens before I have a nervous breakdown.

My phone begins to chirp in the bedroom and I rush in to grab it before I miss the call.

"Hello?"

"Hey, Em," my brother replies through the other end.

"Hey, too!! We still on for lunch today?"

"Yeah, about that, I think we need to seriously sit down and talk, Em. Can I just come over? I really don't feel like having this conversation out in public."

"Riley, what the hell are you talking about? What conversation can't we have in public?" "Em, I'll talk to you about it when I get there. I'm leaving a work site right now, thanks to your husband. He sent me out of town and I'm about two hours away from you."

I start to say something back to him, but the line disconnects.

What the fuck was that all about? Why would Keith send him out of town and then pull him from another crew?

Things are really starting to get fucked up, and sooner or later I'll have to intervene.

I go back to the bathroom and dry my hair, pull my eyeliner and mascara from the basket and apply my makeup. I head back to the bedroom and grab a pair of shorts and a tee shirt to get myself dressed.

Since I have all the time in the world now, I decide to tidy up the house and start some laundry.

After about two hours I'm finally done folding and putting away the last load. *Shit, I hate this tedious chore.*

By the time I make it downstairs the doorbell is ringing. I open the door to the disheveled shell of my little brother.

"Riley, what the hell happened to you?" I ask, moving to the side for him to come in.

He shakes his head while walking into the house. Riley pulls his Red Sox baseball cap off his head and runs his fingers through his short brown hair. He looks over at me with his hazel eyes, both trimmed with the same redness I just saw in my own a few moments ago.

"Come on, let's go to the kitchen and I'll make us something to eat."

I move toward the kitchen and hear his footsteps following me.

"Is a sandwich okay?" I ask.

I reach into the refrigerator and pull out some cheese and cold cuts.

"Yeah, it's fine. Do you have any of those sweet gherkins?" he asks, looking over to me with sad puppy dog eyes.

I nod my head and smile at him, "I even have your favorite sour cream 'n onion chips, too.

"You know, you really are the best big sister, Em. You remind me so much of Mom that sometimes it hurts," he says, taking a seat at the kitchen table.

"I miss them a lot, too, Riley."

"Do you think I'm more like Mom or Dad?" he asks with a sad look on his handsome face.

"I think you are a lot like both of them, Riley, and they would be proud of you no matter what."

I drop the conversation on that note and busy myself making us each a plate of turkey and cheese sandwiches with a pickle and a handful of chips.

"Can I get you something to drink?"

"Yeah, water's fine. Thanks, Em."

We sit in silence as we eat our lunch, but the curiosity of what he wants to talk about is killing me.

"So, what's going on that you needed to come here to talk to me about?" I ask, looking across the table at him.

He sets down his bottle of water and pushes his empty plate away from him.

"Em, I'm having a real issue with the way things are being run at RPK Contracting and today was the straw that broke the camel's back."

"Why? What happened?" I ask, having no clue what's been going on between Riley and Keith.

"Your fucking husband is what happened! Ever since Mom and Dad passed away he's run that place like it's his own. I've gotten cut from all of my crews but one and now I've lost *that* crew as of this morning."

"What? How?"

"Em, I don't want to put you in the middle of this, I really don't. It's bad over there and I don't know what to do anymore. Last week I confronted Keith and told him I thought it was time for me to step in as part owner. I went to the bank and tried to take out a loan to buy him out, but I couldn't get approved. I feel like everything I ever wanted is now gone, all because of your asshole husband."

I put my head in between my hands and lean forward. I said from the start I didn't want to get into this between them, but now I feel like I don't have a choice. I know Riley is hurting and he's my brother. I also know that my husband is running my father's business, and if I choose to take Riley's side it could ruin everything my father worked so hard to create.

I have a serious decision to make on what I want to stand behind. Either way, I'm going to hurt one of the most important men in my life. I never thought it would come to this, but now there is too much at stake for me to step back. I need to do something before the three of us lose it all. If Mom and Dad were here things would be so much different. Unfortunately, they aren't and I'm the one who has to make one of the most difficult decisions of my life.

I look up at Riley—he's so sad, he's hurting—but there's only one thing I can do to make all of this right. I just need to find the strength to do it knowing very well I will lose him in the process.

Chapter 11

Emma

My nerves are peaking with what I'm about to tell my little brother. Knowing how hurt he's been about losing his part of the family business is one thing, but I think I'm about to break his heart all together. I know it has to be done, I…no *we* can't risk losing the business because of his faults. As much as he wants this to be his, it's not worth the troubles he's been causing.

I will stand by my husband and pretend to be the perfect wife. I'll do whatever it takes to keep RPK Contracting running smoothly; it's the least I can do for my parents. It's the only thing I can do to keep their memories alive in this community. They were such a valuable asset to this town and loved by so many. I can't have their name dragged through the mud because Riley is making errors on the job.

On nervous, wobbly legs, I get up to stand from the table and grab our empty plates. Standing on the other side of the kitchen I look over at my brother who is now gazing out the window.

I wish I knew what was going through his mind right now. I have no clue what's gotten into him or why he'd jeopardize the reputation of the family business. We are both grieving over our loss, but he still has no excuse to throw away his job.

It's now or never; I have to say something. My hands are shaking and my stomach is in knots. I can almost feel my lunch getting ready to come up and make an appearance all over the tile floor.

"Riley," I say in almost a whisper.

He looks over at me and nods his head.

"I know that things have been tough since Mom and Dad passed away, it's been really hard on all of us. Have you ever thought about stepping back from RPK for a while to see what else is out there for you?"

He looks at me with shock on his face.

"What the fuck did you just ask me?! Leave the business, or should I say what's left of it, altogether?"

Pure anger comes across his face, and for the first time in a long time I don't know how my brother is going to react to what I have to say next.

"Look, Riley, I sure as hell don't want to cause an argument with you. I'm just saying with the lack of accountability you've had, it's no surprise Keith has taken crews away from you."

"Really, Em? Seriously! Are you fucking kidding me right now?!" he screams at me, throwing his hands up in the air. "I've done nothing but bust my ass on these crews and your fucktard of a husband is pulling me off my jobs. I haven't done a damn thing wrong. I know this business in my sleep and would never do anything to destroy what Dad and I worked so hard to create."

"You're obviously upset right now, Riley, and I can see that. It's just that I don't know if this is the kind of business you should be in anymore. I mean without Dad here it seems like you've fallen apart. We need someone to run RPK Contracting like Dad would have and right now I don't think you're the guy for the job. For Christ's sake, Riley you're still a kid. This is a serious business, do you really think you can be half the man Dad was at your age?"

As the words come out of my mouth I see the sword being pushed further into my brother's heart. It's too late to take it back; it's been said, and by the look on my brother's face, there's no way I'll ever be able to erase the words from his memory.

He moves to stand from the table and slams the chair against the wood.

"I'm glad to know how you really feel, Em. All this time I thought we were a family and would be able to get through these hard times together. Obviously I was way off. Well, don't worry, I won't burden you or your precious husband ever again. Don't worry about showing me to the door; I don't want you slamming it against my back on the way out. Good luck, Em, I hope you and your thief of a husband have a happy life together taking away what was rightfully mine."

Riley grabs his hat from the table and storms out of my house.

I can't move; my feet are like two blocks of cement. My mouth is hanging wide open. I'm hurt, shocked and at a loss from the conversation I just had with my little brother. Never in a million years would I have thought things would have ended this way. I mean, I knew we would argue, but I didn't think he'd be hurting this badly.

There's no point in running after him. As much as I wish I could've said something else to let him know how I was really feeling, it's out in the open now.

I listen as Riley's tires screech against the wet street in front of our house. With all the rain we've had the past few days, and the fact that it's now getting darker, I hope he's careful.

Good God, what have I done? I should've just stayed in bed today. I knew there was a reason I felt the way I did.

I begin to move my unstable legs and make my way back up to my bedroom. If nothing else, I can lie back down in my bed and drown in a puddle of my own tears. Not only do I have a husband that barely talks to me, but I just lost the only other man in my life that meant the world to me.

I curl up on my bed and pull the afghan over me that my grandmother had made for me and as a wedding gift. Closing my eyes, the last thing I see is the hurt in my brother's hazel eyes.

My phone starts to chirp and I reach my arm around to find it. After searching through the covers, the noise finally stops.

I quickly sit up in my bed and look around my room. It's now dark and I have no clue how long I've been sleeping. Looking to the bedroom window, I see that it's still raining and now completely dark outside. The clock on Keith's nightstand shows it's well after seven o'clock.

Shit! I've been napping for more than three hours.

I finally find my phone on the floor and check for my last missed call.

The phone starts to chirp in my hand. I don't recognize the number, but I still accept the call.

"Emma," a male voice says.

"Yes, this is Emma."

"Hey, it's Ted from the club."

"Umm, hey Ted," I respond with uncertainty to my voice.
"Er…umm…Keith's not here. You may want to try his cell phone. Do you need the number?"

"No, Emma, Keith is here with me and the guys at the Batting Yard down on Wilson Avenue. Well actually, he's passed out on the floor. It seems that Riley and Keith got into an argument and your brother beat the shit out him. I don't know if it was the beers packing the punches or what, but your hubby is banged up pretty bad. You might want to get down here and get his ass to a hospital."

"Are you kidding me right now, Ted, 'cause this really isn't a joking matter."

"No, Emma, get down here as quickly as you can. We have him in the back office, but like I said, he may need medical attention. At least a few stitches if nothing else."

"I'll be right there and thanks for calling, Ted."

This is fucking unbelievable and I hate to think that it's entirely my fault.

I quickly gather my thoughts and hop out of bed. Running down the stairs, I pull on a pair of flip flops and head out the door.

The entire way over to the Batting Yard all I can think about is if I would've handled things differently with Riley this wouldn't have happened.

I pull up to the bar and park in one of the front spots. As I'm walking to the door Ted comes out to meet me.

"Hey, Emma, good to see you, sorry you had to come down here like this. We tried to clean him up the best we could, but he' still knocked out cold."

I look over to him and wonder why a room full of grown men couldn't help a friend out by taking him to the hospital.

I shake my head at him, "Where is he so I can get him home?" I ask in a bitter tone.

"Follow me," he replies.

He takes me back to a hallway of closed doors. When he opens the last door on the right, a sight appears before me that I didn't expect.

"Holy shit!" I scream. "You guys should've taken him to the fucking hospital, not called me to come here."

I look at my husband lying on the cold tile floor of a bar room office.

His face, neck and shirt are covered in blood. For all I know his nose and jaw are broken.

"Emma, we didn't know what you would have wanted us to do. If it were me lying on the floor, my wife would have wanted to be called first."

"Well, thank God I'm not your wife, Ted, because I would be kicking your ass right now. How the hell am I supposed to get him to the hospital by myself?"

The two guys standing behind Ted must sense my anger; I'm sure as hell not holding it in.

"I'll call for an ambulance."

"Too little too late now, assholes," I say through clenched teeth.

I crouch to the floor and attempt to wake Keith. After a few attempts of trying to wake him, he finally comes to and opens his eyes.

"Keith!" I yell. "You have some serious explaining to do, but right now I need to get you to the hospital. The guys here will be coming with me because there is no way in hell I can pick you up if you fall down."

He nods his head, but doesn't utter a word.

I point to the two guys behind Ted, "You and you, get your asses over here and help him up. Ted, help them get him in my car and follow me over to General Pines—that's if you're sober enough to drive."

"Yeah, Emma, I'm good. I think the shock of all this has killed my buzz by this point."

"Too fucking bad for you," I reply. "Maybe the next time four grown men walk into a bar they'll be smart enough not to get into a fight. Where the hell is my brother, anyway?" I look between Keith, Ted and the two other morons in the room.

"He took off after he gave Keith here his award winning knock out. Lucky for him, he left without a scratch on him."

"Does anyone know where he went?" I ask.

The three guys shake their heads no and Keith just mumbles nonsense.

"Ugh, you're *all* worthless, do you know that?"

Climbing to my feet, I brush off my hands and knees. I follow close behind as the three guys attempt to assist my dumbass of a husband out of the bar and into my car.

This honestly cannot be happening to me.

Mom, wherever you are, please give me the strength to make it through this night without killing one of these four men. God only knows the thoughts that are crossing my mind, and when I get a hold of my brother there will be serious hell to pay. I don't care what the hell has happened in the past few hours, this is unacceptable.

Chapter 12

One week later

Saturday August 11, 2012

Emma

The past week I've been living in hell.

Ever since the fallout between Riley and Keith, I've been walking on eggshells in my own home. The slightest look in the wrong direction is setting Keith off and my cell phone rings nonstop with calls from my brother.

I'm exactly where I don't want to be: stuck in the middle of these two men.

No matter how much Keith says Riley attacked him that night at the bar, I still don't understand what would make him so angry that he'd go off like that. Riley's never hurt so much as a fly; it was all so out of character for him.

Keith felt so defensive about the whole fight that he banned Riley from RPK Contracting all together. If Riley so much as steps foot on the property or a crew site, he's to be immediately removed.

In my opinion, Keith has taken things too far, but with everything else going on I'm keeping myself out of it. Not only is Keith pissed off about the actions my brother took against him, but he's livid the way I treated his friends at the bar. I feel like I'm in an episode of the Twilight Zone and there's nowhere for me to escape.

Thankfully, some of the ladies from the club were meeting for lunch, and after much hesitation I decided to join them. It was nice to get out and socialize with a group of old friends, that's until I'd had enough of them. Hearing their happy love stories and plans of summer family vacations started to piss me off. Feeling self-pity is one thing, but having these ladies drudge up the latest gossip about my life was enough for me. After a few hours of cucumber sandwiches and cocktails I decided to head home and organize my life.

When I pull up to the driveway, I see Keith's car parked in the garage and a sick feeling starts to form in the pit of my stomach. I hate the fact that just the thought of him churns my gut.

I know deep down I love my husband, but after all we've been through the past few months I honestly can't stand the sight of him anymore. I feel as though I've been living with a different man. He's rarely ever home and when he *is* there's a constant argument about something.

I've been trying to get into RPK Contracting for the past few months to go through Dad's office, but for some reason or another Keith wants me nowhere near the place. Legally, this business is mine, too; I have every right to come and go as I please.

Our sex life has taken a turn for the worst again, but this time I don't mind the lack of attention from him. In fact, if he were to come on to me, I'd either have to fake it or find a way to get out of it.

I let out a heavy sigh, pull my car into the garage and make my way inside.

Lucky for me, when I walk into the kitchen, I see Keith asleep with the TV tuned to a baseball game.

The emotion of sadness and loss is so overwhelming for me. Not too long ago we would've had a house full of friends and family here to watch the game. So much has changed in our lives and I know better than anyone that it will never be the same again. My parents are gone and my relationship with my brother is nonexistent.

It drives me crazy how quickly things have gone bad for our family. I hate to say this, but it all started shortly after Mom and Dad passed away. Things would never have ended up like this if they were still here with us.

Yeah, Keith and I had issues after the news of our infertility, but we were able to work through it. It really wasn't until *after* the accident that things took a turn for the worse. It all started after the will reading—when we found out Riley wasn't given a part of the business. Ever since then, Riley and Keith have been at each other's throats.

I just don't get it. They've always gotten along, that is until Keith took over RPK. He's been leading on for the past few weeks that Riley was the cause of so many issues, but…wait a minute, is it Riley that's really the issue or is it Keith? I walk toward the front window and see Riley's Durango sitting in front of the house.

I walk out the front door, careful not to make too much noise and wake up Keith.

As I walk down the front lawn, I watch Riley get out of the car.

I raise my hand in the air to gesture him to stop.

"Emma, I need to talk to you."

"Riley, don't. There's enough trouble going on between you and Keith right now. I don't want it brought into my home now, too."

"Emma, you need to let me explain what happened. It's not right that you only know his side of the story. I know that if you let me talk to you it will all make sense."

I shake my head.

I can't do this anymore.

"Riley, what you've done to us—to me and Keith—is unforgiveable. I need for you to turn around and leave. Please don't call me, Keith or the business anymore. You've changed, Riley, and I don't know what's gotten into you, but you're not the brother I once knew and loved."

I turn my back on him and walk back up to my front door.

Tears begin to stream down my face and it hurts so much to have to say goodbye to my little brother. He's right, though. I only know Keith's side to the story, but for now that's all I need to know. I saw what Riley did and there were others that saw it happen, too.

He needs to get on with his life without me in it. I love him and will always think about him, but for now our family is torn. I need to focus on me right now, not the struggles my little brother is creating.

I open the front door, turn to shut it and watch as Riley drives off down the road. I shut the door, slide down to the floor and break down into a fit of tears.

I hate what's happened to me—to my family—and there's nothing I can do about it. I lean my head back against the door and close my eyes.

"Em! Em! Emma!" I hear Keith screaming my name and I open my eyes.

Shit, I fell asleep on the god damn floor in front of the door.

Keith is standing over me and looks down at me like I'm crazy. I guess if I saw him in this position I'd think the same thing.

"What the hell are you doing sleeping in front of the door?" he asks with a scowl on his face.

"Umm, it's nothing," I say, moving myself to stand up next to him.

He wraps his arm around my shoulders and a tremor runs through my body. He walks us toward the living room and pulls me down onto the couch next to him.

I want to run away and scream; the last thing I want is to be sitting next to him. I need an excuse to get up, like now.

"Hey, you hungry?" I ask, moving to stand.

He pulls me down into his lap and his lips find mine.

Ugh, this is so wrong. How awful is it that I can't enjoy intimacy with my husband? I need help, *serious* help.

I pull away from our kiss before he takes this a step further.

"Come on, Keith, I'm starving. You want me to make you something?" I ask getting up from his lap and walk toward the kitchen.

"Yeah sure, whatever you're having is fine with me."

"Okay, give me a couple of minutes and I'll have something fixed right up."

I busy myself in the kitchen making a quick dinner. The further away I can get from him right now the better. I don't know what's wrong with me, but there's no way in hell I'm in the mood for sex with him.

I finish making the sauce just as the pasta is about done.

Out of the corner of my eye I see Keith walking toward me. I turn my back to face the stove and tense as his arms come around my body. He grazes his lips against my neck and a sudden chill runs through my body. He's kissing the most sensitive part of my body, yet the feeling I'm getting in return is nothing like it used to be.

I push back against him to move, but he takes this as a moment to advance on me. He turns me in his arms and crashes his mouth to mine. His kiss is urgent and hard against my lips. As much as I want to fight him right now, I don't know how to get out of it. If I push him away he'll very well know that I don't want any part of him.

He deepens the kiss, sliding his tongue into my mouth. I hate this so much I almost want to bite down on his tongue and pour the scalding hot water over the top of him.

The buzzer to the oven begins to beep and a huge sigh of relief takes over me. My entire body begins to relax as I try to move away from him. He pulls away from our kiss for a brief moment to turn off the oven and lifts me onto the counter top.

"I want you so bad, baby. Tell me you want me, too," he says, looking up into my eyes.

"Keith, I…"

He doesn't give me another moment to speak and takes my head in his hands pulling me forward to resume our kiss.

I'm so distraught—so emotionally drained—that I give in to him and let myself go. Hell, it's just sex with a man I've had sex with a million times over the past ten years.

I wrap my legs around his waist and pull him in closer to me until I can feel his body against my core.

My mind begins to drift to a better time, when Keith and I were happy. At one point I wanted to be back there with him, but now I don't know what our future holds.

He lifts me off the counter with one arm and turns toward the stove to shut off the burners. Walking us to the living room, he lays me down on the couch.

Keith's lips find mine instantly as he undoes the button on my shorts. He moves his hand under my tank top and lifts my bra to free my breasts. His lips travel down my neck to my collar bone, and in one quick movement, Keith has my tank up and over my head.

I close my eyes and take myself back to my happy place. If I'm going to enjoy this moment with him, I have to pretend that we're back to the way we were before all of this happened.

I lose myself in my own mind, paying no attention to what is happening right here and now. Before I know it, Keith has removed all my clothing and is pumping himself in and out of me while he rubs my sensitive nub.

I buck my hips to meet his every move, and within a matter of seconds we both come as our climax takes over our bodies. I open my eyes and look up at the man I used to love—the one that had my heart above all else—but now the man I see looking back at me is not that man anymore.

Chapter 13

Monday August 13, 2012

Emma

Keith and I drive onto the interstate and a giddy feeling courses through my body. Today is finally the day I'll get to do what I've wanted to do for months.

"You sure you'll be okay while I'm gone? Keith asks me for the hundredth time this morning.

I look over at my husband as he drives his truck to the airport.

"Keith, I'm a grown woman and it's not like you're ever home now anyway."

"I know, but I'll be gone all week. I hate thinking you'll be all by yourself."

"I'll be fine, I promise. Call me when you're not on site and I'll give you up to date feedback on my wellbeing."

He lets out a laugh and grabs for my hand. He interlocks our fingers and squeezes my hand.

I don't know if it's the sudden business trip or the fact that he realizes how wrong he's been treating me, but he's been overly attentive with me since Saturday night.

Since our wham-bam-thank-ya-ma'am sex session the other night, he's wanted to be near me more often.

Honestly, I've given in to him more than once since Saturday night.

The sex between us has always been great, and since when do you have to feel connected to a person to sleep with them? Hell, if he brings me to orgasm every time we have sex, I promise not to complain ever again.

He pulls my hand to his lips and places a gentle kiss to the center of my palm.

"I'll miss you while I'm gone. Don't do anything crazy without me," he says, wiggling his eyebrows.

"Oh please, Keith, you're the one going off on a business trip. I'll just be stuck here in Greensboro cleaning house and doing laundry."

"Well. You know you can still come with me if you want to."

"No, I would just be bored out of my mind while you're on sites; it's best for me to just stay home. Plus, you're only going to be gone four days; you'll be back before you know it."

"Yeah, I guess you're right."

We pull up to the departure gates and Keith gets out of the truck. He comes round to my side and opens the door. Leaning into the cab of the truck, he places a soft kiss to my lips and reaches into the back seat for his suitcase.

"I'll see you Friday night; don't forget to pick me up."

I give him a smirk and giggle.

"I'm serious, Em, I don't want to be left stranded here."

"Knock it off, you fool, I won't leave you stranded. I'll see you in a few days. Go show them what RPK Contracting is all about and get us some big jobs."

He smiles at me and leans in for a goodbye kiss.

I watch as he walks up onto the sidewalk. He turns to look at me for a split second and I wave goodbye as he walks toward the building.

I shut the passenger's door and slide over into the driver's seat. I buckle my seatbelt and put the car into drive.

It's time to do some much needed work that I've been trying to do for months. With Keith on his way out of town, the time couldn't be more perfect.

I turn back onto the interstate and head to my dad's building. RPK is my family's business and it's time I stood my ground and found out what's been going on since my father's death. I feel kind of bad sneaking around Keith's back to check in on Dad's office, but I hate the way he pushes me away when I'm there. I have this nagging feeling that he's hiding something and it's about time I figured out exactly what it is.

I did a lot of thinking and soul searching yesterday during my run. It's been well over five months since my parents' death and I don't know that I've handled things the way I should have. I tried getting in touch with Riley, but his number has been disconnected. I went over to his apartment, but the neighbors said he moved out a week ago. I hate the way I treated him the last time we spoke. Now he's gone and I have no clue where he is or how he's doing. I'm his big sister—the only family he has left—and I pushed him away.

I twist and turn through the roads of town until I come across the industrial park that houses the tall brick building of RPK Contracting. I feel like it's been years since I've been here, but really it's only been a few weeks.

I pull Keith's truck into Dad's parking spot and head into the building. I'm immediately greeted by Christine, the receptionist on the first floor. Her cheerful personality is contagious and I find myself smiling from ear to ear throughout our entire conversation.

I make my way up to the second floor and my nerves are a bit on edge.

When I get off the elevator I see Joanne, Dad's secretary, sitting behind her desk on the phone. She sees me walking toward her and lifts her finger indicating that I should wait a moment.

I take a look around the room and notice that nothing much has changed since I was last here. The photos on the walls make me smile as I see the various jobs and completed projects that my father took part in over the years. This place may have started small in my parents' kitchen, but over the years it's grown into one of the most reputable contracting companies on the east coast.

"Emma, sweetie, what are you doing here today? Keith should be on a plane right now, he's not here," she says, coming around her desk toward me.

She pulls me into an embrace and squeezes me.

"It's so good to see you, too, Joanne. I actually just dropped Keith off at the airport. I know it's been a while since I've been up here, but I wanted to go through some of Dad's stuff. I haven't had a chance to clean out his office and I figured now was as good a time as any."

"Of course you can go in there. If you need anything or if I can help in anyway just come out and let me know."

"Thanks, Joanne, I will."

I walk away from the reception area and move toward Dad's office. My heart starts to race and a queasy feeling overcomes me. I have no clue what it is that I should be looking for, but at the same time, I'm determined to go through the entire office until I find something that Keith could be hiding from me.

I turn the knob to the office and enter the room that was a second home to my father.

The room, for the most part, looks the same as it did when Dad was here. The black wooden desk is still off to the side facing the giant windows. There are bookcases filled with family pictures and a few chairs scattered amongst the room. I notice that it looks much cleaner in here than it did when Dad worked in this room. *Figures that Keith, the neat freak, would have order even at work.*

I sit down at the desk and toss my purse onto the floor. Sorting through all the drawers, I don't seem to come across anything out of the ordinary. I rummage through the file cabinets, but all I see are documents and plans for past and upcoming job sites.

Fuck!

I look over toward the bookcase and see a picture of Mom, Dad, Riley and me from last summer. A tear slowly trickles down my cheek as I think back to the day this photo was taken. As I lift up the frame, I notice a black box sitting against the back of the case.

I set down the photo and pull out the box.

The top of the black box is engraved with my dad's initials. It almost looks like a cigar box. I open the lid and inside is a golden key with a tag on it that reads #143.

I pull the key out of the box and examine it between my fingers. It looks too small to be a house or car key. I don't know if it would fit into any locks here in the building. If it was for the business, though, why would it be in a box?

Whoever put it here sure as hell didn't want anyone finding it.

I'll need to do some more investigating to see if anyone here knows what the key is for.

I put the box and picture frame back onto the shelf and take one last glance around the room.

I tidy up some of the things I've moved around and leave the office.

When I walk back out to the reception area I see that Joanne is off the phone and working on some paperwork.

"Hey Joanne, did Dad ever mention a key to you like this?" I ask, pulling the key out of my pocket and handing it over to her.

She looks at it for a few moments and then the tag.

"No, I've never seen this before. It doesn't look like something that we'd use here. At least I don't think so."

"Yeah, I found it in the office and I'm not too sure what it would belong to."

"Hey, hang on a second, there's something stamped on the back of the key. Look here," she says, pointing to a stamp of some kind.

The marking is so small that I can barely make it out.

"If you can find a magnifying glass you may be able to read what's imprinted on it."

I take the key back from Joanne.

"Thanks for the help, Joanne. It was so good to see you again."

"You too, sweetie, don't be such a stranger and stay away so long. We don't have many women around here and it's nice of you to stop in every now and then."

I give her a warm smile and make my way back toward the elevator. I place the key back in my pocket and head back down to the first floor.

A few faces I don't recognize come onto the elevator as I'm getting off. It's kind of crazy to see people here that don't know who I am. My father wanted this to be a family run business where everyone knew one another. I can see that's one thing that Keith has changed.

I walk toward the front desk and see Christine talking with a man that looks to be wearing a security guard uniform. I roll my eyes at the thought that Keith still has security here for fear that Riley may come back and kick his ass again.

I walk up to the desk and wait for them to finish their conversation. Christine looks over to me and smiles.

"Hi, sorry to interrupt, but I was wondering if either of you recognize this key. I found it in Dad's office, but Joanne and I have no clue what it could be used for."

Christine takes the key in her hand and looks it over.

"Sorry, Emma, I don't think it's for anything in this building. The majority of the locks are now all electronic; we don't really use keys for much of anything."

"Do you mind if I take a look at it?" the guard asks.

"Yeah sure, go ahead."

"It looks to be a key for some sort of lock. Did your father have a storage unit of some kind or a garage?"

"I don't think so, at least not that I *knew* about."

"I would check with some of the local storage places around and see if they can help you."

"I'll do that, thank you so much for your help."

Making my way back to Keith's truck I feel like I could be a step closer to finding out what this key could be used for. I have no clue why there would be a storage unit, especially since Mom and Dad had a huge house that could fit just about anything.

I may be leading myself on a wild goose chase, but I have all week to figure this out before Keith gets back home.

Chapter 14

Wednesday August 15, 2012

Emma

Damn it to hell, another failed attempt. I've been to just about every storage unit in Greensboro and no one seems to know what this key could belong to. Throwing in the towel sounds rather appealing at this point.

It's just about dinner time and I know Keith will be calling in soon to check in. I feel like a two year old the way he's treating me. The more overbearing he's become, the more I want to know what this key will open. I have this sick sense that he knows what I'm up to, and once I find out what's been going on, all hell is going to break loose.

There's one more storage place I want to hit before I head back home. It's a bit out of the way from where I'm at—and from the sounds of it, a little run down—but hell, it's worth a shot. Thank God for the old man at Rent A Space. He was so helpful looking up storage units around the area and drawing me up a map.

I punch in the address to my next destination and head toward the interstate. It's about thirty minutes from where I'm at so I blast the radio and begin my journey.

After about twenty minutes on the road, I hear my phone start to chirp from the center console and I activate the hands-free option on my phone.

"Hello?"

"Hey, baby, how are you?" Keith asks.

"Hey, I'm good. How was the meeting today?"

"Ehh, it was good. I think they have a serious interest in what we can do for them in a reasonable time frame."

"That's great, Keith."

If nothing else, he's getting us more work for the business.

"Yeah, I'm about to head back to the hotel and grab some dinner. What are you up to?"

Shit, I can't tell him what I'm actually doing. Damn it to hell, I hate lying. That's the whole problem I'm having with him right now. Honesty really is the best form of communication, but I can't let him know what I'm up to until I have something to tell him.

"Oh, I'm just running some errands. There's this thing I've been dying to check out so I'm searching all over the place for it."

"Sounds like you've been pretty busy. Well, I won't keep you much longer. Give me a call when you get home."

"Okay, will do."

"Talk to you later, baby. I love you."

"Yeah, you too, Keith, bye."

The line disconnects and I exhale a huge breath of air.

At least I didn't totally lie to him; I just didn't tell him exactly what it was I that I was looking for.

I look on the navigation screen and make my final turn toward the storage place.

I pull my car into the parking lot and make my way to the office. It appears there's no one at the front desk. A bell sits on the counter, and as much as I hate to use it, I really don't have all day. I hit the bell and a few moments later a female comes around the corner.

"Hiya, sugar," she says in an overly upbeat tone.

"Hi," I reply. "I was wondering if you could help me with something. I found this key and didn't know if you knew whether or not it would fit one of your units."

"Well, hand it over honey and let me take a look."

I hand her the key as she puts on her glasses from on top of her head. She inspects it, smells it and even licks it. *What the fuck?*

"Yeah, sugar, this looks to be a key to one of our larger units down around back. Are you the owner of this storage space?" she asks, looking at me quizzically.

"Umm, well, technically no. I believe it belonged to my parents who passed away a few months ago. I have power of attorney over their assets so it shouldn't be a problem."

"Let me look up the actual owner to this unit before we go down. I don't want a stranger going into someone else's things."

Well isn't that awfully nice of her? At least she won't be wasting either of our time.

I watch as she pounds on the computer keyboard.

"Hmm," she mumbles looking up at me. "What was your father's last name, honey?"

"Kincaid," I reply.

"Well that's odd; this unit is in the name of Keith McIntyre."

No fucking way. Why the hell would Keith have a storage unit without me knowing? I knew he was up to something, but this is ridiculous.

"Err…well…umm…Keith is my husband," I stutter.

"Oh, okay, that works, too. Do you wanna still go take a look at it?"

"Yes, please. I've been looking all over town for the unit this key will open. I have no idea what could be inside, but I need to know."

"Okay, let me toss on some shoes and we'll go take a look."

I shake my head as she walks around the front desk in a totally mismatched outfit.

Dear God, this lady is batshit crazy and I'm about to walk with her to the back storage unit.

I follow her as we exit the office and walk around to the larger storage units. I watch the doors as we walk by and see the numbers getting closer and closer to #143. Standing in front of the storage unit, I'm feeling giddy and nervous to see what's behind the closed door.

I watch as she fumbles with the key trying to put it into the lock. She's such a mess that I'm about to ask her if she wants help. I see the lock pop off the hinge and fall to the floor.

"Ahh, there we go," she says with a laugh.

As she begins to lift the door my eyes go wide.

"Holy fucking shit!" I shout aloud.

My hand comes up to cover my mouth and I pick my jaw up off the floor. I walk forward toward the inside of the large storage unit.

The first thing that comes into my sight is a large bass boat. I walk along the side of it and see that it's filled with fishing gear and life jackets. As I walk closer toward the back I see a motorcycle.

I look back to the lady and see that she' still standing there watching me.

"Umm, I'm good here if you want to go back on up to the office."

"Oh, okay, well here's the key and you're more than welcome to come in anytime you like."

I give her a smile, "Thank you."

I continue looking through some of the things along the back wall. There are tools for job sites, boxes filled with stuff from my parents' house and items that look to have been in my dad's office.

I have no clue why Keith would be hiding all of this stuff in here. *Was this all my parents', or is it his, and why the hell would he have it locked up here?*

I start to make my way out when a shiny silver lock box catches my eye. I walk over to the wall and pick it up off of a tool chest.

This is crazy weird, all of the original stickers are still on it.

I say a silent prayer, hoping that the box will open when I pull on the latch. If there's another random key out there I'm going to flip my lid.

I set the box back down on the tool chest and lift the lock. I move to pull the top off and thank God it opens. The lock box is filled with documents. I pull out the stack of papers and begin to rummage through them.

The title and registration to both the boat and bike are in here along with a stack of other things. I look over the registration and see that these two items belonged to my mom and dad.

When the hell did they buy a boat and a motorcycle?

I laugh to myself at the image that is now plastered in my mind. Mom and Dad riding down the highway on their brand new Harley…yeah not so much.

I begin to sort through the mess and can't believe what's lying in front of me.

An updated will from December 2011, the deed to the property, the land and the full rights to the business lay in front of me. My mouth is once again open as my jaw hits the floor.

How is any of this possible?

I pull my head into my hands as I shake it back and forth.

All this time he knew and he hid it from me. He lied and hid an important part of my life from me…his wife.

That stupid motherfucker. How could he, why would he…..ugh the nerve!

I need a moment to digest all of this.

I slam the lock box shut and make my way out of the storage unit. Pulling the door back down, I place the lock back on the hinge and head back to the car.

I can't believe what I've just found. I don't know what to make of it or where to even begin to process it all.

Placing the key back in my purse, I walk to the truck and head for home. My head is spinning and I'm not too sure what to make of any of this.

The business isn't mine—it sure as hell isn't Keith's, either. Every piece of it—the land, the building and RPK Contracting—is all Riley's. God, I wish he was here; I need to tell him. I have to find him, but how? He's left and I have no idea where he went.

The ride back to my house is a complete blur. I'm not sure what to do or how to approach this with Keith.

I know once I confront him about it, things will get crazy bad. I'm disappointed, hurt and I feel like the man I once knew has been playing me for the past few months. Things have been bad between us before, but this is it.

I don't know how I can even look at him, let alone be in the same room with him.

Pulling into my driveway, I maneuver the truck into the garage and walk inside.

I toss my purse onto the table and grab for a bottle of wine from the refrigerator. My emotions are so all over the place I need to feel numb for a few hours until I pass out. I pop open the bottle and pour myself a nice big glass of Moscato. I carry my glass and the bottle into the living room and turn on the television. I find myself a good movie, sit back onto the couch and down my first glass of wine.

As the cool liquid passes through my lips and goes down my throat I feel myself slowly beginning to calm down.

Tomorrow is a new day; it's the start of a new me. I will begin my mission to destroy the man that broke my heart and stole my life.

Chapter 15

Two weeks later

Thursday August 30, 2012

Emma

My alarm goes off at seven o'clock and I slam my hand down on my nightstand trying to find the cause of this incredibly dreadful beeping sound. I finally find my cell phone and touch the snooze button. I wrap myself back up in my sheet and fall back into a peaceful sleep for another eight minutes.

My eyes open and my ears start to ring from that god forsaken beeping sound. I dig my phone out from under my pillow and touch the alarm button.

Ugh, damn it to hell. I hate this stupid running schedule.

Swinging my legs out of bed, I glance over to the flat sheets and pillows on the other side of the bed that haven't been disturbed.

I've been sleeping like a baby thanks to Keith's crazy new schedule and his absence in the bedroom.

He's been either out of town or falling asleep on the couch pretty much every night since he came home two weeks ago. He's been working extra hours at RPK Contracting and went back to South Carolina yesterday to finish up some last minute deal for a huge mall down in Charleston, South Carolina. Having him gone is the best thing that could've happened to us. I've been sweating bullets trying to figure out how I wanted to approach him about all of this, but before I do I want to make certain all my ducks are in a row.

When Keith is around I've become so accustomed to faking just about everything; it's now become completely natural for me to act as the 'new Emma'. I've never been the type of person to tell so much as a white lie and now I've become a liar and a manipulator. I have to remind myself daily that this is for my family. I'll do whatever I have to so that I can make things right again for me, Riley and Mom and Dad.

This last trip to Charleston will let us know whether or not Keith and his crew will need to relocate for the next few months. He doesn't seem to mind the time we're apart as much as he did before and he rarely questions my whereabouts when he's not here.

My fingers are crossed that he'll be spending more time away from home in the near future. I need this distance from him to keep myself sane and not slip up. Our relationship is definitely torn, but for now I don't mind it at all. I'd rather have him out and about busting his ass for my family's business that driving me crazy here at the house.

While getting dressed and ready for my run, I smile to myself. I'm quite proud of what I've been able to accomplish in a short amount of time. I've located the lock to the suspicious key, scanned and copied all of the documents in the lock box and put the copies back to their original spot. As of right now, Keith doesn't know I've found his secret stash and I need to keep it that way for a little while longer.

I took all of the documents over to the family attorney, Mr. Bryant, last week. With his help we've been able to sit down and review all of the items in the lock box. Thankfully, he was able to quickly determine that RPK Contracting rightfully and legally belongs to Riley.

My next struggle is to find my little brother. It's the mission that I'll be focusing on starting next week. Until then, I have to get my ass in gear and go for a run.

I make my way downstairs, grab my armband and head out the garage door. Today I have to run at least six miles and my goal is to do it in under an hour. With my Spice Girls remix blasting in my ears, I know my girls will help me get it done.

Well, shit, here goes nothing. I start off with a slow and steady pace. Once I hit mile three I pick up speed a bit, but not too much to make me burn out early. For the next two miles I average a nine minute mile which isn't too bad. Mile six starts and I know that I'm now in the home stretch. I pump my legs a bit faster and start to see the roof of my house come into view. I move into a sprint, determined to get this last mile down in less than eight minutes.

I reach the bottom of my driveway and feel as though I could collapse. *Fucking hell, whose dumbass idea was it to build our house on top of a hill?* I slowly drag my tired ass up the pavement and take in slow easy breaths until I regain a normal breathing pattern. I pull the armband off to check my mileage and time.

Hell yeah; I just ran six miles in less than fifty minutes.

Even though I'm completely spent from my run, I muster enough energy to do a happy dance through the garage and into the house. On the way past the fridge I grab a bottle of water and a banana from the counter.

It's already going on eight-thirty and I still need to shower and head over to Mr. Bryant's office to drop off the original documents.

I'll feel much better knowing that they're in his hands and not lying around here for Keith to find.

As much as I want this to all be over and done with, I need to maintain my 'good wife' appearance until all of this is settled. It could take weeks or even months, but I'll do whatever I can to make this right again. Mom and Dad would want it this way and I can guarantee they are rolling over in their graves because of what Keith has done to me and Riley.

Marching my way up to the bedroom, I eat my banana and gulp down my water. Once I'm in the bathroom, I toss out the peel and set the bottle down onto the countertop. I strip myself of my running gear and head into the shower. Letting the hot water run over my now sore muscles, I enjoy the feel of the hot steam surrounding my body.

After what feels like forever under the water, I finally wash my hair and body.

Once I'm feeling fresh and clean I turn off the water and step out of the shower to dry off.

I glance at the time on my cell phone. *Shit, it's almost quarter after nine. Time to bust a move.*

I finish drying off, dry my hair, apply some makeup and move into the bedroom to get dressed. It's hot as hell outside today so I choose to put on a pair of khaki shorts and a black tank top.

Heading back into the bathroom, I give myself a once over in the mirror and grab my cell phone. I have just enough time to make it over to the attorney's office before our scheduled appointment.

I rush downstairs grab my purse and head out to my car. Pulling the manila envelope out from under the driver's seat, I set it on the seat next to me.

In record time I make it over to Mr. Bryant's office.

As I walk into the building, he's standing at the front desk talking with Patty, his receptionist.

"Well good morning, Mrs. McIntyre," he says, extending his hand to me.

"Please, call me Emma," I reply extending my arm to shake his hand.

"Come on into my office and we can get started."

I wave good morning to Patty and follow close behind him.

As we make our way through the door he turns and moves behind me to close it.

"Were you able to get everything we needed for today?" he asks.

"Yes, I made copies of all the documents and placed them back into the lock box. Everything that we went through the other day is all in this envelope. Now, if I could just find my brother, we'd be all set to move forward."

"Nicely done, Emma," he says with a smile.

"Yeah, I feel like this has been the easy part; living with someone you despise is the hardest thing to do right now.

"As I told you before, I can get you in touch with a reputable divorce attorney."

I give him a smirk.

"I know and I will take you up on that sooner than later. I just want to make certain that nothing goes wrong until Riley is aware of what's going on with all of this."

"You just give me the word when you're ready."

"I will. Thank you so much for all of your help over the past few days. I feel like I've been living in a nightmare. I just want it to all be over with. Starting Monday, I'm making it my next personal mission to find my brother. Once I'm in contact with him, we'll start to put things in motion."

"No worries, Emma, I respected your father a great deal and I hate what Keith has done to your family's business. It will all be made right again, you just need to be patient."

I hand him the envelope and watch as he files it away in the cabinet against the wall.

"It's in good hands here, Emma, don't worry."

"Is it that obvious?"

"Pretty much. Honestly, if you need anything please let me or Patty know."

"Will do, thanks again. I'll be in touch."

I turn from him and walk out the door and into the parking lot toward my car. I feel a sense of reassurance knowing that the original documents are out of Keith's reach and that we're one step closer to getting back the family business.

I hop into my car and start on my way back home.

I know Mr. Bryant said I need to be patient, but holy hell, I want this misery to end now, not later.

My phone starts to chirp from my purse and the number on the display screen isn't one that I recognize. I hate telemarketers and I'm not really in the mood to talk to one this early in the morning.

Feeling like a bit of a rebel, I hit the hands-free button on my steering wheel and answer the call.

"Emma," a voice says.

Oh my God, it's Riley.

"Riley," I reply with a twinge of excitement to my voice.

"Hey…um…I…um. I'm down here in Greensboro on business and really wanted to know if there's any chance I could see you tonight," he rambles.

I'm so excited to hear him I could scream.

"Riley! It's so good to hear your voice. The way we left things was absolutely horrible on my part, but you have to understand, I don't think I've been in my right mind since Mom and Dad died."

"Emma, you're my sister, and no matter what's happened over the past few weeks, I'd like nothing more to move past it all with you."

"Oh, thank God!" I screech. "Where are you staying while you're down here?"

"I'm in the Embassy Suites by the airport. Can you come by and meet me for dinner? I'd rather it be just us though for tonight. I want to talk to my sister without distractions and interruptions. To be honest, Emma, I really don't think being around Keith is a good idea."

Oh shit, he has no clue how bad it's going to get.

"I understand, Riley. I can be over that way around six-thirty tonight."

"Good, thanks, Emma. See you then," he says and disconnects the line.

My heart is racing and I can barely think. He's back—well, not technically back—but I have him here for one night. It's my chance to make things right and tell him what's really been going on with me, Keith and RPK Contracting.

This should make for an interesting reunion for sure.

Chapter 16

Emma

My nerves are all over the place as I drive over to the hotel Riley's staying at tonight. I don't know what I'll do when I see him. Do we just say hi, shake hands, lean in for a hug? I hate that it feels so awkward meeting my little brother for dinner, but then again we didn't leave things on the best of terms.

I have so many questions I want to ask him. Where did he move? Where is he living? Does he have a job? Is he eating right?

Ugh, I feel like a mother hen.

I pull into the parking lot in front of Embassy Suites, and honestly, I'm feeling a bit sick to my stomach. I'm not sure if it's the fact that I'll be seeing my brother after what happened or that I'll be telling him what I've recently found.

I sit in my car for a good twenty minutes zoning out before I realize what time it is.

Shit! It's after six-thirty. I need to get inside the restaurant before he thinks I've stood him up. I don't need to piss him off more than I have already.

I step out of my car on wobbly legs and make my way toward the hotel. I look around the lobby and steer my way to the restaurant. My heart is pounding to the point that I feel like my hair is about to stand on end.

I glance around the tables in search of Riley and spot him standing next to a table. I raise my hand to wave and walk toward him.

"Hi, Emma."

He extends his arms in front of him and a warm feeling spreads from my heart all over my body. *I need to relax. This is not going to turn out bad; it's going to be amazing.*

"Oh, Riley, I'm so sorry. I've missed you so much!"

I lean into his embrace and hug him as tight as I can.

"I know it's only been a few weeks, but I feel like I haven't seen you in years," he says, pulling away and taking a seat at the table.

"I know, me too. I don't want this meeting to be awkward between us. You're my baby brother and I want to know how you've been since you left," I reply, taking a seat across from him.

"I agree. I'm just glad you came," he says with a smile.

Seeing him again makes me feel so happy. Even though we're ten years apart in age, we've grown quite close to one another in our adult years. It's just not the same not having him around all the time. I miss our banter, his sick and twisted jokes and the way he can turn any topic of conversation into a comedy show.

I watch his every move. His hazel eyes are no longer trimmed in red and the smile on his face tells me that he's happy.

I know I need to share my news with him; I just hope I don't freak him out in the process.

"So Riley, I need to talk to you about something I found after you left. I know I should've tried to find you, and I probably would've built up the nerve to do so sooner or later, but there's some stuff you need to know. But first, and don't argue with me, tell me where you've been living and what you're doing now."

He looks at me with a playful glare and I can tell what's brewing in his head. I may be bossy at times, but I want to make sure he's been okay before I drop this huge weight on his shoulders.

"Typical Emma," he says with a wink.

"You know it, now spill," I reply with a smile.

He squirms around in his chair and sets his hands down in front of him on the table.

"Well, I moved up to Boston a few weeks after I came to see you. I'm living with a guy that had an ad on Craig's List. I'm dating a girl I met at a mini-mart. And I'm working for a contractor."

Shit, could he have given me any less detail? I guess I should've pried a bit more, but now the punkass is giving me the bare minimum. He's such a little shithead, but I'm still so happy to be sitting here with him again.

"Well played, Riley. I hope your short story really isn't as creepy as you just made it sound and I hope you're happy," I say, staring into his eyes.

It's kind of scary how well my brother and I can communicate just by looking at one another.

We're interrupted for a few minutes while the waiter approaches our table to take our order. It's moments like this I can appreciate. I needed a second to take everything in and breathe.

"So, does Keith know that you're meeting with me tonight?"

I let out a heavy sigh and swallow hard.

"Actually, no he doesn't. He doesn't even know what it is that I've found. I've thought a lot about how things were handled after you left, Riley. I'm embarrassed to say that while mourning Mom and Dad, I treated you so unfairly. I let Keith walk all over the both of us so that he could fulfill his own need to run the business. Things are really going to change and I needed to tell you first."

I look into my brother's eyes and my heart starts beating out of control.

"Emma, what did you find that you need to tell me about?" he asks in a nervous tone.

I start to fumble with my napkin on the table.

"Well, don't freak out. Okay?" I'm really getting nervous now.

His eyes begin to squint and he runs his fingers through his short brown hair.

"Emma, you can't start off a conversation like that and *not* expect me to freak out."

"Fine, Riley, don't piss me off," I pause for a second to take in a deep breath, "So, after you left I went to RPK's headquarters and tried to clean out Dad's office. Keith had been working in it the past few weeks and really didn't have the time to go through a lot of the paperwork. So I decided I could do a little housecleaning for him. After sorting through some things I found a key."

"A key to what?"

"At first I wasn't sure—I didn't know. It didn't fit into any locks in the building, and it looked too small for a house key, so I started to ask around. Turns out it belonged to a storage unit not far from Mom and Dad's house."

"What? Why would they have a storage unit when they owned a huge house and a business?" he asks with a tone of pure confusion.

"That's what I thought, too. I went down later that night and checked it out. Riley, it was filled with stuff that neither you nor I would have ever known they had. I don't know what the hell they were doing with all the stuff and why it wasn't in the house."

I can tell he's dying to know what I've found, but this isn't the easiest of conversations to have. Regardless of the outcome, I hate what has happened, and to know my husband is the cause of all of this just makes me sick.

"Emma, what did you find?"

"Well, at first it was just big stuff like a bass boat, a motorcycle and some big tools to use on jobs. Stuff like that. But then there was a lock box. A brand new lock box that still had the original labels on it and everything."

"Come on, Emma, you're freaking me the fuck out. What was in the lock box?" He's starting to raise his voice.

Oh shit, he's getting pissed off at me. As much as I want to blurt it all out, I'm scared he's going to be upset with me for not telling him sooner. I lock my eyes onto his.

I let out another breath of air. *It's now or never.*

"The deed to the business, the land, the building—everything belonging to RPK Contracting was in this lock box, Riley."

"Okay, so what's the big deal? We had all of that with the will," he says, looking at me like I'm an idiot.

Ugh, come on, Riley, use your fucking brain. Don't make me spell this out for you; it's hard enough to tell you as it is.

"No, Riley, you don't get it. It was an updated deed of *everything* and it all has *your* name on it."

His mouth drops to the table and I can see that he's at a loss for words.

He clears his throat. "Emma, what does that mean?"

Good God, Riley….pay attention…think!

"Riley, it's all yours. RPK Contracting is *yours.*"

The look of shock on his face is priceless. There's no doubt in my mind, I've shocked my little brother and he's now speechless.

Just as luck would have it, our dinner arrives and we're forced to eat the food setting in front of us.

While we eat our meals we talk a bit more about the items I found in the storage unit. I let him know that I'll support whatever decision he chooses to take with his new ownership of the family business. I encourage him to take some time to think things over, nothing has to happen right this second. Even though I hate Keith, he's still doing his job and running the business.

I've clued Riley in about what's been going on with Keith and how I've consulted with Mr. Bryant. He needs to know what's happening and if I want us to remain close I need to let him in on my life again.

After dinner, Riley walks me out to my car. Together we decide to head over to the storage unit in the morning so that he can see everything that's left of our parents' possessions.

On the drive home, I think back on the past few months and everything that's happened to my family. There's no doubt in my mind that I'll *ever* push my brother away again. He's willing to help me in any way he can and even suggested that I can come up to Boston if I need some time away.

It's so good to know that I have him in my life again. I'll need his support to get through these struggles with Keith, especially once I confront him and file for divorce. I wish that Mom and Dad were here to help me too, but as long as I have Riley I know I'll be able to get through this.

I've managed to make it through today and I'm excited to see Riley again in the morning. I don't know if he'll want anything that I've found, but if he does, everything has already been registered and insured under our names. I know I sure as hell won't need anything in the unit, but I'll make sure he knows he's welcome to anything he wants.

I make it home, and without even shedding my clothes, I fall onto my bed.

Tonight I'll be able to sleep so much better knowing that everything is progressing just as it should. I've found my brother and I know we're in this together. My next obstacle is to deal with my asshat of a husband when he returns in two days. If I can keep up this act, I'll deserve the academy award for best and biggest bitch wife *ever*.

Part two
We Met & Everything Beautiful Began

Emotionally drained,

in search of a place to call my home

and find my happily ever after.

Chapter 17

Five months later

Friday January 25, 2013

Emma

    I stare out at the road in front of me and watch as the trees fly past me and the cars and tractor trailers go by in the distance. I've traveled quite a few hundred miles since I left early this morning and still have a way to go before I reach my final destination.

Getting lost in my own thoughts, I start to think back through the past year of my life.

It's been three hundred and thirty-eight days since my parents passed away in that tragic accident.

Eleven months and two days since I heard my mom's voice through the phone telling me we would meet for dinner later that night.

We never got a chance to say goodbye.

It still hurts every day that she's gone, but her sweet voice and beautiful face are etched in my memories forever.

I don't know how I've gotten through half of the struggles I've been through without her. I've seen the tagline, *God only sends you what you can handle*. Well hot damn, I must be a serious badass because all I've been handed is shit for the past several months.

A single tear runs down the side of my face and I remind myself that I need to be strong. Mom would want me to only remember the good times and not dwell on the loss of those we love.

I can only hope that both my parents would be proud of me for what I've done. Even though I may have had to lie and be deceitful, I still accomplished the job I set out to do.

It's been one hundred and forty nine days since I found my brother, or more like since *he* found *me* again. Four months and twenty-seven days since he walked back into my life and forgave me for being a stupid-ass big sister.

I hate the way I treated him. It kills me that I pushed him away when I should've been grieving along with him, but I'm so glad that we're a family again. I've learned so much through my mistakes and promise myself that I'll never take my loved ones for granted again.

I've said goodbye to the shell of a person I was for far too long.

I'm moving on to a new life, a life that's focused on *me*. No longer will I allow others to control how I feel or cause me to hurt those that love me the most. I have an incredible support system and I'll do anything to keep them close and let them know how much they mean to me.

It's been five days since I last spoke to my husband.

One hundred and twenty hours since I've had to see him.

The man that lied, stole and destroyed so much of my life and my family.

He was the person I thought I'd spend forever with, but yeah, not so much now. If only I could have known then what I know now, my life would've turned out completely different.

My last words to Keith will stick with me forever, *"When you said that we'd be together forever, I thought that would mean until the end of time. But I guess forever isn't as long as it used to be."*

He looked me in the eyes, grabbed the pen out of my hand and signed the papers that were laying on the kitchen countertop. Once he was done signing at all the red X's, he slammed the pen down, turned away from me and stormed out the garage door.

I haven't seen or heard from him since. *Good riddance, you stupid fucking asshole.*

I don't know why he was so pissed off at me. Maybe it was the fact that I caught him in one too many lies or it could've been that Riley and Mr. Bryant were standing behind me the whole time. Either way, I got what I wanted: a divorce from the asshat and his resignation from RPK Contracting.

I had known for a long time what I needed to do and I stuck around just long enough for Riley to decide what he wanted to do with the family business. Everything that was once broken is now fully restored. Keith is out of our lives and the business is back in the capable hands of my little brother.

Now it's my turn to focus on me and my happiness. I know it's out there somewhere; I just need to be patient and let it find me.

I don't know what will happen next—or where my journey will take me—but for right now I'm heading to Boston; it's where my support system is located.

Riley has assured me that I have a good place to stay for as long as I'd like. He even said that there will be a job waiting for me at Char's dad's business, Taylor & Sons Contracting, if I want it. With an offer like that, how could I say no? Plus, I get to be closer to my favorite girl, Char.

I never really got to be close with another female, unless you count the snotty trolls at the club. There's something about Char; we click in a way that I never have with another female.

I can see why Riley loves her so much. I'm happy for both of them and excited to see where their relationship goes. Neither one of them is pushing the marriage factor, but I'd love for them to pop out some babies for me to spoil.

I'm ready to put this road trip behind me and get to Boston, but according to my navigation I still have a little over three hours. My legs are getting twitchy and I think my ass fell asleep a few miles back.

This is no 'simple' journey; this has been a fourteen hour nightmare. I should've taken Riley up on his offer to go back with them the other day when he went with the moving truck.

Now I'm stuck taking this God forsaken road trip from hell all by myself.

As much as I hate to stop, I need to get out of the car. The traffic has been pretty good so I think it's about time to pull off for gas and stretch my legs.

I watch the signs and take the next exit turning off at the first gas station.

I'm not too sure where I am exactly, but the last sign said I was nearing Yonkers. I need to make this pit stop quick. It's already dark outside and knowing my body as well as I do, it will want to go into sleep mode. I quickly get out, pumping gas and grabbing a twenty-four ounce steaming cup of caffeine.

Hopping into my car, I hear my cell phone begin to chirp. I start up the car and see Char's name flash on the display screen.

A smile appears on my face and I push the hands-free button.

"Hey lady," I say.

"Hola, chica. Where you at?"

"Ugh, I'm near Yonkers. Wherever the hell that may be."

She lets out a laugh and I can hear Riley yelling something in the background.

"Riley, stop it. Yes, I know, I'll ask her. My God, do *you* want to talk to her?" she mumbles through the phone.

"What's his problem?"

"He's worried that you're going to fall asleep driving. Now these are his words not mine…because you're an old lady. He wants to know if we should meet you so he can drive the rest of the way for you."

"Oh my God, he's such a dickhead. First of all, I'm not an old lady and second, I only have a little bit more to go. Tell your stupid boyfriend that I'll see him in a few hours, but only if his old ass can stay up that late."

"Oh my God, you two are nuts," she says with a heavy sigh.

"What, we're nuts? Nah, you're just imagining things. This is a totally normal conversation for me and my brother. You should know this by now, Char."

"Shit, you two are going to drive me crazy," she laughs.

"I'll be on my best behavior, I promise."

"Em, don't make a promise we both know you won't be able to keep."

"Okay, fair enough, I'll try my best not to make you go crazy."

"Okay good, get your ass up here so we can pop open this bottle of wine I bought today. Plus, I think Derrick has cleaned his house a hundred times so that it's perfect for you."

"I'm trying; I should be there between nine-thirty and ten."

"Yay, drive safe and we'll see you soon."

"Okay, see you in a few hours."

The line disconnects and I return one hundred percent focus on the road in front of me.

I have so much to be grateful for right now.

A complete stranger is about to take me into his home. Granted, it's only a few houses down from Riley and Char, but still it's going to be interesting to moving in with a guy I barely know.

Char and Riley swear that Derrick is a good guy and would do just about anything to help them out. I honestly don't care where I stay as long as I have a roof over my head and a place to sleep at night.

They've given me the condensed story of his life and apparently he's going through a recent break up as well. Between the two of us we should make a pretty damn depressing pair.

Char has described Derrick as a guy with a heart of gold. He's been her best friend for years and just went through a recent break up with his girlfriend that he'd been dating since high school. I made her swear that moving in with him won't cause any issues for him and his ex-girlfriend.

That's when she told me his ex was also her sister….and I thought *I* had drama.

Riley mentioned that Derrick is a lawyer and recently began working loads of hours to keep his mind busy. Having him out of the house and at the firm will give me a little more space that I'll need to find myself again.

The first thing I want to do once I get to Boston is settle myself into Derrick's house. I don't want things to be awkward, but I also don't want to replace his girlfriend, either.

Once all of that's settled, I want to take Riley up on his offer to work for Char's dad. I've gone this long doing odds and ends for RPK; it's time I put my college education to work and start trying to build up a career of my own in project management.

This is a fresh start for me and with everything that Riley, Char and Derrick are doing for me, I'd be stupid to pass up on this opportunity.

I glance to the navigation screen and see that I only have forty-five minutes until I'm there, so I crank up the radio and the first song that comes on is *A Little Bit Stronger* by Sara Evans.

Holy shit, this song could've been my fucking anthem. I listen to the words and pump myself up. I'm grooving to the song in my car knowing that every day I *am* getting stronger. I'll get over the pain of the past year and move on with my life again. I'm making it my personal mission in 2013 to start my life over.

No more listening to what others tell me to do.

No more being taken for granted.

No more living like I don't matter, because I do.

Chapter 18

Emma

It's a little after nine when I finally pull into the driveway at Derrick's house. I'm so tired I just want to close my eyes and fall asleep.

Leaning on the headrest of my seat, I turn off the car and shut my eyes for a quick second.

Just for a moment I need to rest my eyes.

A loud bang pulls me out of my cat nap.

I jump out of my seat and my eyes fly open to see my stupid brother standing outside my driver's side door tapping on the window.

"You stupid jerk!" I scream. "You scared the shit out of me!"

Laughing hysterically, he opens the door.

"Sorry, Em. I took Manny out and saw your car parked in the driveway. Why the hell are you still sitting in your car?"

"Ugh, I just wanted to close my eyes for a second and I must have dozed off."

"Well, that happens when you're up in age. I think it's called a senior moment or something like that."

"Riley, tired or not, I'm going to kick your ass. I'm not old!"

"Leave her alone, Riley," I hear Char say.

"Hey, Char, can you tell your punk-ass boyfriend to leave me alone so I can get out of my car?"

"Babe, come on. Let your sister at least get out of her car before you begin to attack her with your crude banter."

I watch as Riley turns to Char and gives her a kiss on the forehead.

"Anything for you, baby," he says.

"Oh God, I think I just threw up in my mouth."

Char laughs and pushes Riley out of the way.

"Come on, girl, we have a bottle of White Merlot calling our names."

"Oh thank God. I need a glass or two right about now."

I get out of my car and Char pulls me into a hug.

"So glad you made it. This is going to be so good for you, I just know it."

"I know it will; it's just going to take some time getting used to living with a stranger and being in a town I know nothing about."

"Don't worry, Em, we'll take good care of you."

"Let's go introduce you to your new roomie."

I give her a smile and nod my head.

"Show me the way."

I follow Riley and Char into the house and as soon as I walk in I'm greeted by my favorite Bulldog.

"Oh Manny, I've missed you," I say crouching down to him. "Did you miss Aunti Em?"

"Oh shit, you can't deny the craziness of this family," I hear a voice say from the other room.

A tall guy walks around the corner with short brown hair and crazy-bright blue eyes. I stand to say hi, but Manny knocks me back down.

"Manny!" Char yells. "Let Aunti Em go."

"Oh good God, you have your dog referring to her as if she's really his aunt. You know that doesn't make any sense right?"

Oh, I can tell this guy and I are going to get along just fine.

Manny jumps off of me and runs toward Char. I move to stand and Derrick extends his hand to help me up.

"I'd give you a hug to say hi, but you're kinda covered in dog drool," he says with a smile.

"I'm Derrick, by the way."

I smile back at him.

"Yeah, I figured that much. I'm Emma."

He throws his arm around my shoulders and pulls me into his side.

"Welcome home, Emma, make yourself comfortable. I'll give you the grand tour starting with the luxurious downstairs hallway," he says, lifting his left arm in the air.

"Ohh, it's breathtaking," I reply sarcastically.

"Yes, yes it is."

He walks us into the kitchen.

"This is the room where you'll be cooking me all my meals. Not to worry, I have a full list of everything I like on the fridge."

"Smart man," I say with a giggle.

He leads us through the kitchen into the living room.

"Here, we have the place where I'll be watching all of my television shows and you'll be bringing me all my favorite snacks and beer."

"Ahh, I see," I say, trying to refrain from busting out in laughter.

"See guys," he says, turning us around to face my brother and Char. "We *are* going to get along just fine."

"Yeah, I can see that," Char says with a smile.

"The upstairs isn't as fancy as down here, but you will have a cot, a bucket to piss in and use of the shower once every other day."

Char walks up to Derrick to smack him on the chest and grabs my hand, pulling me back into the kitchen.

"These guys are just full of it tonight, don't mind them. They're not always like this; they just get all excited when a hot chick is around."

"You don't need to give excuses for them, it's okay…really. I think I'll fit in here perfectly."

"I know you and Derrick will get along just fine. Let's grab a glass of wine and sit out back. For once it's not freezing outside and we should take advantage of it."

Char pours us each a glass and we make our way out back.

The four of us sit outside by the chiminea fire and chat like a bunch of long lost friends. It feels so good to have these people here for me and I can't wait to start fresh here in Boston.

"I'll be right back," Riley says, heading back inside.

I take my last sip of my wine and set my glass down on the table.

"You ready for round two?" Char asks Derrick and me.

"Yeah," he replies.

"Okay, I'll go inside and get us each a refill."

"I'll come with you to help. I don't want you spilling any of my wine," I tell her.

I follow Char into the house and hear Riley talking to someone.

We walk into the kitchen and I stop dead in my tracks.

Who the hell is he?

A tall guy is standing next to my brother choking on his beer.

He's hot as hell—not that I'm looking—but holy shit. He has dark hair, blue eyes and he's....*wow*.

Pete

I check the time on the microwave for the tenth time since my sister, Kar, called me an hour ago.

"Shit, Kar, I gotta go. I'm supposed to be over at Riley and Char's house in a half hour."

"Okay, no worries. I just wanted to check in on you," she says in a sweet tone.

My sister is quite overbearing and feels the need to check in on me a few times a week. I get that she's only doing it because she cares, but she could take it down a notch. You'd think I was a child and needed a parent to check in on me to make sure I wiped my ass.

"Kar, I'm good I promise," I say, letting out a heavy sigh.

"Don't you dare huff at me, Pete. You say that you're good now, but I know that bitch is going to be up your ass begging for you to take her back."

"Look, I don't like Kathy any more than you do right now. But I can tell you that it's over. I haven't heard from her in two weeks, I think she's taken the hint."

"All I'm saying is that you can do better, Pete. You're a good looking guy and I want to see you happy."

"I *am* happy, Kar—happy that I'm single."

If she doesn't let up sooner or later I think I might just start banging my head against the wall.

"We'll see how long that lasts. I bet that you'll have another girl on your arm in a month."

"Nope, not gonna do that again. I need some time for me. If—and I do mean *if*—a girl comes along, I'll just keep on walking. No, better yet, I'll start *running* in the other direction."

"Okay, Romeo, you do that. Have fun over at Riley's house. I'll call you sometime next week."

"Sounds good, love ya, Sis."

"Love you, too, Pete."

We disconnect the line and I grab my keys from the kitchen counter.

I shake my head as I look at the time on the microwave again. *Nothing like being late to a surprise welcome home party.*

This chick coming isn't even *from* Boston; I don't understand why Riley's calling it a welcome home party. I'm not exactly sure what the hell is going on, but Riley said I needed to come over and get out of my funk.

My friends and family are just a bunch of morons; I don't get the need for them to babysit me. I'm not, nor have I ever been, in a funk over some chick. Yeah, my girl and I broke up. Big deal, it happens all the time. Live and learn and get the fuck over it. Simple as that. There's no need to dwell on it. If they'd back off I can guarantee I'd get over the bitch much faster than if they keep bringing her up. It's actually starting to get on my nerves.

I slide into my truck, crank up some Blink 182 on my XM radio and hit the road.

It's a little after quarter to ten when I pull into their development. I turn the corner to Derrick's house and see a car parked in his driveway. I pull in behind it, my lights shining on the baby blue car.

No fucking way. This chick has a Mini Cooper convertible with a white soft top.

I let out a loud laugh and turn off the truck.

This is going to be epic; she's gotta be something to drive a girly car like that. How the hell is she Riley's sister?

I get out of the truck and slowly walk past the priss-mobile and onto the front porch. Before I can ring the bell Riley is standing in the doorway.

"What the fuck, dude? I told you to be here at nine. It's almost ten o'clock."

"No, you told me nine thirty, so I'm only a few minutes late."

"Shit, did I screw up?"

I shake my head and push him out of the way.

"Where's my girl?" I ask, looking around for Char.

I love the way it pisses Riley off every time I hug her.

Looking around the kitchen, I don't see anyone. Riley comes in and opens the refrigerator, pulling out two Miller Lite longneck bottles.

"Everyone is out on the deck," he says, gesturing toward the other side of the house.

"Sweet, thanks, man. So, where's Char?" I ask, wiggling my eyebrows.

I pop the top from my beer and take a long sip.

"Dude, shut the hell up. Leave my girl alone. She's got all she needs right here with me," Riley says pointing at himself.

I laugh so hard the beer almost flies out my nose.

"Oh, I see Pete's here," Char says, walking into the kitchen with her hands filled with two empty wine glasses.

"Hey there, pretty lady. You know I came here just to see you."

"Yeah, I'm so sure," she rolls her eyes and giggles.

My eyes dart from Char to the figure standing behind her.

Holy shit, who the hell is this?

A girl walks in behind Char, and believe it or not she's shorter than Char, but damn she's hot.

She has long brown hair that reaches to her mid back, eyes to kill a man and lips—good God those lips.

"Umm…yo…Pete, pick your jaw up off the floor for a second," Riley says, smacking the back of my head.

She walks straight toward me and extends her petite hand in my direction.

"I'll assume you're Pete. Hi, I'm Emma," she says with the sexiest Southern accent.

"Well, you've assumed right. It's nice to meet you," I say, grabbing her hand in mine.

She smiles and looks up at me with the most amazing hazel eyes I've ever seen.

Riley nudges me in the side.

"Don't even think about it," he says, giving me a glare.

Char gives Riley a smirk and grabs Emma from me and moving them toward the counter to fill up their wine glasses.

I nod my head in his direction and make my way out to the back deck to get a breath of fresh air.

"Hey man," Derrick says as I step out onto the deck.

"Well, you got it made, man."

He lets out a laugh, "Yeah, why's that?"

"Umm, have you seen your new roommate?"

"Who, Emma?"

"No, the other fucking chick in there with Char. Yes Emma, you dumbass."

"I don't know, Pete; she's Riley's sister. I'm not doing that to him *or* her."

"Yeah, okay. You both just broke up with your significant others. You can't tell me that if she came crawling in your bed you'd kick her out."

I watch as Derrick's eyes glance behind me. I shut my eyes and shake my head.

"She's standing behind me isn't she?"

"Yep," Derrick replies.

I turn around to see Emma and Char both standing behind me—each with one hand on their hips and the other holding a glass of wine.

"Shit, sorry, I didn't realize you were standing behind me."

"Yeah, I can see that. Not to worry, no one is tapping this ass or kicking me out of their bed anytime soon."

"You tell them, girl. You need to start fresh here in Boston, not get dragged down by a bunch of assholes," Char says, glaring at me.

I throw my hands in the air, "What did I say?"

Chapter 19

Emma

Char and I take our glasses of wine back into the living room and cozy up on Derrick's leather couch. She taps me on the leg and I look in her direction.

"Well *that* was interesting to say the least," she whispers.

"Yeah, I didn't think I'd get comments like that thrown at me on my first night here." "Don't mind Pete, he's really harmless," she says.

"He seems like a total dick. How do you guys know him anyway?"

"Nah, he's not normally like this. He's just…well, I don't really know what's gotten into him tonight. I've known him forever. He works for my dad and is the head of building design for Taylor & Sons Contracting. He works on the lead crew with Dad, Riley and two other guys."

"Ahh, I see," I reply, giving her a questionable smirk.

"Really, he's a good guy. If he wasn't, I don't know that Riley and Derrick would hang out with him. He just got out of a really bad relationship a few weeks ago. The girl he was dating was a complete bitch and he found out she was cheating on him with some guy she worked with. It was pretty bad for a while. That's why Riley wanted him to come over tonight. Pete's been laying low for a bit and we thought it would be good for him to chill with us."

"Well. I'll give him the benefit of the doubt tonight, but if I catch him pimping me out to Derrick again *I'll* have to smack him upside the head."

Char lets out a laugh, "I'd pay to see that."

I gulp down the last sip of my wine. *Damn, this is going down way too smooth and I'm beginning to feel it already.*

"You want another glass?" Char asks.

"Yeah, I'll have one more. Then I think I'll call it a night; I'm getting pretty tired."

"Hmm, I wonder why. It's not every day you take a fourteen hour road trip."

"True, and I don't plan on making that trip again anytime soon."

"Well, let's go fill up our glasses and I'll show you the upstairs."

Char and I move to the kitchen for a refill and head up the stairs.

The room I'll be staying in is already furnished from when Riley was staying here. Derrick's even set it up with new curtains, bedding and a few pictures of Boston.

It looks so welcoming in here. The colors are awesome; I don't know that I could've done a better job myself.

"Geez, Derrick really went all out in here," I say, looking around the room.

The walls are painted in a crème color, and there is dark brown wooden furniture set up throughout the room. The curtains are a deep purple that match the crème and purple bedding. It's perfect.

"You can't give him *all* the credit. I did a final sweep to make sure it looked okay," she says with a smirk.

"Well, you both did a great job. I can't thank you guys enough for doing all of this for me."

I don't know if it's because I'm so tired, or the wine, but I'm beginning to feel a little emotional. I sit down on my new bed and stare at the wall of pictures featuring my new home.

"Hey girl, what's wrong? You look like you're about to cry. What happened to the happy-go-lucky Em?" she asks, sitting down next to me.

"I don't know, Char, it's just a lot to take in right now. I thought I had my whole life planned out for me and now I have no clue *what* direction I'm going."

She wraps one arm around my back and leans her head onto my shoulder.

"I can't imagine how you're feeling right now. I mean, I dealt with an ass of a boyfriend before I met Riley, but it was nothing like what you're going through right now. Just know that between the guys and me you'll have all the support you need. It won't be easy, but we'll try our best to make this feel like home to you."

As much as I'm trying to contain the tears, they begin to fall down my face.

"I just want to be me again, Char. It's been so long since I was happy and did things that I wanted to do."

"I know, girl—but don't worry—everything happens for a reason, right? You were meant to be in Boston with us, and starting tomorrow your new life will begin. I have a whole day planned for us to tour Boston. I'll show you all best place to eat, shop and relax if you want. You'll see; it's going to be great."

"I love your optimism, Char. I promise I'll snap out of this funk soon enough."

I look to her and smile, wipe away my tears and give her a hug. I never had a sister to talk to, but if I did, Char would be my choice.

"Good. Now, dry your eyes and let's go back downstairs to harass the guys."

"Sounds like a plan. Thanks again, Char," I say with another smile.

She leads me out of my bedroom and toward the bathroom next to my room, grabs a washcloth from the linen closet and runs it under the water in the sink.

Without even asking her for help, she's taking care of me. No one other than my mom has ever cared enough to help me like this.

I watch in the mirror as she wipes the dried tears from my cheeks and removes the trail of mascara around my eyes.

"There, now you're good as new. No more tears, lady. The new Em doesn't cry over stupid shit anymore; she's way too strong for that. Besides, I think you need a little banter between the guys to pick up your spirits."

I let out a laugh, "Yeah that sounds like exactly what I need to bring a smile back to my face."

"Then let's get our asses downstairs," she says, tossing the washcloth into a basket next to the sink.

As we walk down the stairs I see the guys standing around in the kitchen. Once we're in their sights Riley strolls over and scoops Char into his arms.

"There you are. I was about to send a search party up there for you," Riley says, pulling Char into his side.

She nuzzles the side of her face into his chest as he leans down to kiss her forehead.

"Could you two please contain your public display of affection? You have three broken hearts watching here and it's no fun," Derrick chimes in.

"Umm, speak for yourself, Derrick. There's no broken heart in this girl; I'm happy to have said good riddance to that asshat."

I look over to Pete as he spits his beer out of his mouth. The four of us burst out laughing at him.

"Well then, this girl has her priorities straight," Pete says, wiping the spilled beer off of his shirt.

I give him a wink and take a sip of my wine.

Char is right; my new life starts now and no longer am I going to cry over the pain of the past.

Pete

Stupid putz!

I can't seem to keep my alcohol in my mouth tonight when Emma's around. If she didn't think I was an ass before, she sure as hell will now.

She's kept her distance from me ever since she overheard me talking to Derrick out on the deck. I don't want her thinking I'm a dick—well, it's probably too late for that—but still, I'd like to get to know her if she plans on sticking around here for a while.

I can't help but watch her every move.

She's a tiny little thing, but there's something about her that I can't quite figure out. Her smile is contagious and the way her eyes shine when she looks at me—fuck, it's hot as hell.

If only I could catch her alone for a few minutes, I could apologize and set the record straight. I'm really not the kind of guy to act like this; I don't know what the hell is wrong with me. I'm a thirty-seven year old single guy. I should really get my shit together.

"Hey guys, I know I have a kitchen to die for, but you think we could move our little party into the living room?" Derrick asks, nodding his head toward the other room.

"Yeah sure, come on, Em," Char says, pulling Emma by the hand.

Once again, my eyes dart toward her and watch as she walks away.

"I can tell that I'm never going to see my girlfriend again now that Em's here," Riley says with a pout.

Char turns around and blows Riley a kiss. These two really know how to make a guy's stomach churn.

"Could you two get a room?" I ask with a scowl on my face.

"Aww, are you jealous, Pete? Is someone getting more action than you?" Emma asks me with a cute smirk.

"Oh shit! She told you!" Derrick says with a laugh.

"Well at least she's talking to me now," I say giving her a wink.

"I'd have no problem talking to you as long as you're not trying to hook me up with my new roommate. No offense, Derrick."

"None taken. Em. You're going to be the sister I never had, so no worries about it," he says, plopping down in his leather recliner.

"Glad we got that cleared up, but what about me?" I ask.

"What about you, Pete?" Emma asks.

"Well, we have the lovebirds over there, you and Derrick are roomies. Where does that leave me?"

"I'd say that leaves you out of the loop and shit out of luck pal," Riley says, taking a seat on the couch next to Char.

I watch Emma as she covers her mouth trying not to laugh.

"Thanks, *ass*, I know when I'm not wanted."

"Aww come on, Pete, these three have taken me in. I'm sure they have enough room in their big ol' hearts to give you a little bit of love, too."

"Thanks, Emma, I feel all warm and fuzzy now. I think I'll take a break from this bonding moment and step outside for a bit," I say as I walk out the patio doors and onto the deck.

Manny trails behind me and I take a seat on a chair next to the chiminea fireplace. I stare off into the dark woods behind Derrick's house.

A lot of shit has gone down for me in the past few weeks—but Emma's right—I *do* have some amazing friends that are here to help cheer me up. It drives me nuts to think about what Kathy did to me. After three years, I don't understand how she could've gone and done the things she did.

I don't know if I'll ever want to trust another chick again, let alone let myself open up like I did with Kathy. I gave her everything but a stupid fucking ring on her finger and she moved on without me. No communication, no signs, not one single thing that led me to believe she was having an affair.

I sit back on the chair and close my eyes. I need to move on from the pain she's left me in—at least *try* to move on. I'm not some pansy-ass that's going to dwell on the past, but shit, this still kind of hurts.

I hear the door creak and I open my eyes.

"Would you mind some company?" Emma says in her sweet southern voice.

I sit up in the chair and pull out the one next to me for her to sit. It's dark outside, but with the light of the chiminea I'm able to still see her.

"Thanks," she says, sitting down.

"No problem."

I look back toward the woods, trying to think of the right thing to say to her. I wanted a moment alone, and now that I have it, I don't know what the hell to say.

"I don't judge you for what you said earlier," she says.

I look over to her. She's curled up on her chair and has her feet tucked beneath her.

"Are you cold?" I ask.

"Ehh, just a little."

I take off my fleece and lean over to wrap it around her shoulders.

"Thanks, Pete," she says, grabbing for my hand.

I let her hand rest on mine for a second, but quickly draw it back.

"Damn, Emma, you shocked me."

She sits up in the chair. "Oh, I'm sorry."

"No need to be sorry, Belle, it just caught me off guard."

She lets out a giggle, "What did you just call me?"

"I called you Belle, you know, because you're a sweet southern belle."

"Well thanks, Pete, no one's ever given me a nickname other than Em. My parents always called me Emma, and as for Riley, well that depends on his mood. Sometimes I'll be Em and others he'll call me Emma. But I like Belle; it's different."

"Yeah, that's me—different."

"Don't be so down on yourself, Pete," she says, reaching her hand on top of mine.

Zap.

"Shit, you shocked me again."

"Oops, sorry. I'll keep my hands to myself. It must be from the cold weather and your fleece."

We laugh together for a second.

"I need to apologize for the way I talked to Derrick about you earlier. That really isn't me; I was just being a dick. Lately the things that come out of my mouth are more brash than I'm used to, so I'm sorry."

"Thanks for that, it means a lot."

"So can we be friends now?"

"I'd say that's a good start. Not knowing anyone or anything about Boston, I need as many friends as I can get."

"Good deal, Belle, now I don't feel like the loner in the group."

"You'll never be a loner when I'm around, Pete. I got your back."

"I think that's the cutest things I've ever heard, in a weird sort of way."

For the next few moments we both lean back in the chairs and just stare up at the sky.

I'm glad that I had a chance to talk to her on our own. She's right, having as many friends around as you can is a good thing.

Chapter 20

Sunday January 27, 2013

Emma

It's only been two days living in this new place and already I feel like it's home to me.

I will say, I'm not used the amount of attention I've been getting from Derrick, Char and Riley, but it's still nice to know that they're all here to make me feel loved.

Char wasn't joking when she said we were going to tour all of Boston—well, at least the shopping district.

I got to see so much of the city and I think that I'll start to know my way around in no time. I just need to get myself lost in order to find my way back home again.

The day started with Riley and Derrick waking me up to go for a nice long run around Pier Park. It was cold as shit, but Char was sure to give Riley some cold weather running gear for me to use. It wasn't exactly what I'd planned to do at seven-thirty on a Saturday morning, especially after downing a bottle of wine, but the scenery was beautiful.

After the run with the guys I came back, showered and got dressed for a fun filled day roaming the streets of Boston.

Char took me for breakfast at a cute little coffee shop and then we were off to shop. We took a break and stopped for lunch—my treat that time—and afterward we did some more shopping. Since it's a lot colder up north I was in need of a real winter coat, boots and a shitload of other stuff. Once we were done buying out the stores we came back to Derrick's house for some more food.

The guys cooked us up spaghetti and meatballs for dinner. I was a little apprehensive when I heard Riley was involved in the cooking process, but Derrick assured me that he manned the stove and left Riley in charge of setting the table.

It was another nice, quiet night amongst my Boston family.

I couldn't be happier with the decision I made to leave North Carolina. As much as I miss my dream house and the warm weather, I know bigger and better things are to come for me.

Now I'm lying in my nice warm bed, not having the least bit of motivation to get my ass up. It's only seven, but I have a feeling the guys will be in here any minute to rain on my relaxation parade.

I hear the front door slam shut and Manny's nails scratching along the wooden steps. I turn over in my bed to see his little black nose sniffing under my door. I laugh and throw my blankets off of my warm body.

"Hang on, boy, Aunti Em is coming."

I start to walk toward my door when it bursts open with Manny rushing for me and Riley close behind.

"Well good morning to you, too, Manny. You need to tell daddy that he needs to stay at his own house until at least midmorning; you're lucky I'm not a grouch before my first cup of coffee," I say, giving Riley a look.

"I can't help it, Em. It's been forever since we lived this close to one another. Besides, Char is still sleeping so I had to find someone else to bother. She *is* a grouch before her first cup of coffee so I let her go until she comes to me."

"Nah, I can't imagine Char ever being a grouch," I say, sitting back down on my bed with Manny.

"Give her time, Em, you'll see the real Char soon enough," Derrick says, walking into my room in a pair of grey sweatpants and a Harvard Law hoodie.

"Geez, can't a girl get any privacy this early on a Sunday morning?"

"Nope," both Riley and Derrick say in unison.

"Thanks, guys, next time I'll just lock the door so y'all can't come in." I stick my tongue out at them.

"Go ahead, we'll just pick the lock and get in anyway," Riley says, bending down to tie his shoe.

"Any who, what's the plan for today? Or do I get a day on my own to explore the city?" I ask, looking between the two guys.

"You sure you want to go out alone?" Riley asks.

I look over to him and give him a questionable smirk.

"Let me remind you, little brother, I'm a thirty-eight year old woman. I think I can handle a big city on my own."

"Holy shit, you're thirty-eight. You're even older than Pete and that's old," Derrick says, taking a seat on the desk chair.

My head whips in his direction and I give him a death glare.

"Okay, you two out of my room....*now*," I say pointing toward the door.

"Oh shit, now you did it, Derrick," Riley says, backing out of my room.

Derrick just sits on the swivel chair laughing.

"Umm, that means you, too, Derrick. You want to call me old then get the hell out of my room. I don't come barging into your room at the ass crack of dawn and insult you."

"But Em, you look amazing for thirty-eight," Derrick says through his laughter.

"Derrick, I know I just met you, but if you don't get out of my room, so help me God I'm going to kick you in the balls."

"Okay…okay," he says with his hands in the air. "Damn, she might even be worse than Char without her coffee. Get your ass downstairs and make her a mug of coffee before she cuts off our balls."

"You two really know how to make a girl feel like shit," I say, slamming my door in their pitiful faces.

I really need to get out of this house.

Reaching into my suitcase for a bra and panties, I make my way over to the bags of clothing I just bought. I dig out a pair of jeans and a brown sweater with a white camisole and lay them down on the bed with a pair of socks and my new boots.

This should keep me warm enough for my little adventure today.

Grabbing my robe, I walk out of my bedroom and into the bathroom for a quick shower.

Finally, a moment of peace and quiet, no interruptions and no crude banter.

I let the hot water hit me in the face while washing my hair and scrubbing my body.

Turning off the water, I step out of the shower. I dry myself off and start working on my hair. Once I'm done, I apply some make up and get dressed and ready to go. I grab up my new Columbia coat and head downstairs.

I see the guys sitting in the kitchen and give them a wave before heading out the door.

Tomorrow I really need to get myself organized. Riley moved all of my personal belongings from NC into a storage unit and I could really use some of my things here at the house. But until then, I'm going to enjoy a nice day all by myself.

After being surrounded by this crew for two days I need a breather; if nothing else, just a day alone to sort through my thoughts.

Today is a day for me.

Pete

I need to get out of this house; I can't deal with staring at these walls for another day.

God, is it Monday yet?

It's pretty sad when I'm sitting here wishing the weekend away so that I can go back to work.

My mind needs to be kept busy; if not, I find myself bored and dwelling on the past.

Since the breakup with Kathy, I keep thinking about shit I never thought about before.

I was always the guy that put work and my career before my personal life. I'm good at what I do and I've got one of the best crews on the east coast.

Yeah, I may have taken my work a bit too seriously at times and possibly took advantage of the fact that my relationship with Kathy would stand the test of time. But hell, after dating and living together for nearly three years, who wouldn't?

The thing I don't get is if she wanted more, whether it be my attention or a stupid damn ring on her finger, why didn't she talk to me about it before going off and fucking another guy?

Why can't people communicate? Is that too much to ask?

Now I'm stuck looking back on my thirty-seven years of life, wondering what I have to show for it.

Damn it, this is why I need to get out of here.

I grab my keys from the table and head out to the garage. I step up into my truck, back out of the garage and head down my driveway.

I'm not quite sure where the hell I'm going, but I need to go somewhere. I start to drive through some of the town and decide to head into the city. Maybe walking through the crazy busy streets of Boston will help me clear my mind.

Before I merge onto the highway, I decide to stop at a coffee shop to grab some breakfast.

I pull along the street to park the truck and head inside. Walking up to the counter, I order my usual medium black coffee and a toasted everything bagel with cream cheese.

I pay the gal behind the counter and wait for my food. I glance around the small shop and my eyes stop on her. She's not looking in my direction, instead she's sipping on a mug of coffee and reading over a map of the city.

Her long dark hair is lying perfectly along her back. She's wearing a soft brown sweater that clings to her petite body. Her legs are crossed and she has on some seriously hot as hell boots. *Holy fuck.*

"Pete," the gal behind the counter calls my name and Emma's head pops up.

We make eye contact for a second and I turn around to grab my order.

Shit, I shouldn't have turned away so quick. I should've waved, no, that's dumb. I should've said hi.

I grab my bagel and turn around to see her looking in my direction. I walk toward her and she smiles.

"Good morning, Pete," she says in that sexy as hell southern voice.

"Morning, Belle, do you mind if I join you?" I ask, gesturing to the extra seat at her table.

She shakes her head. "Not at all, please sit."

"What brings you out this way today?" I ask, taking a sip of my coffee.

"I wanted to take on the city by myself today. I haven't really had a quiet moment since I got here, so I thought I'd be adventurous."

"Well, don't let me stop you," I say, grabbing up my food.

"No silly, you're fine. Sit, stay, I don't mind your company. It's just that Riley and Derrick are up my ass trying to keep me busy. I just wanted a peaceful day without them hounding me to do something. Plus, I kind of like getting myself lost and finding my way back."

I watch as she picks off a piece of her muffin and tosses it into her mouth.

"Ah, I see. Must be why you were just studying the map," I reply, giving her a wink.

She starts to laugh and waves her hand in front of her face.

"Damn you, Pete, you almost made me choke on my muffin."

"Sorry, Belle, that wasn't my intention. You okay?"

She nods her head. "Yeah, I'm good. Just wasn't ready for a laugh at that moment."

"Okay good, I'd hate to have to give you the Heimlich if you were choking."

She lets out a laugh. It's soft, but oh so sweet.

"So, back to you and your map. What was it that you were studying?" I ask before taking a bite of my bagel.

"I was trying to find where I wanted to go today. There's so much to see in this city, I didn't know where to start first."

"Well, if you want I can point out some things that you might like to go see."

Or I could just go with you.

"Yeah, that would be great. Unless…well, if you'd want to go with me."

In mid bite I look up at her. *Did she just read my fucking mind?*

She's looking at me with the most adorable look on her face, those hazel eyes shining right back at me.

I swallow the lump of bagel in my throat and grab for a napkin.

"You want me to go with you?" I ask, clearing my throat.

"Well yeah, I mean no…well, if you have other plans that's fine, too. I just thought since, well never mind."

Damn she's even cuter when she gets flustered.

"No Belle, actually it's a great idea. I was thinking of heading into the city myself to clear my head. I've been sitting in my house like a lump on a log and needed to get out. I just stopped here to grab some breakfast."

"Great, well looks like we're starting out the right way. We'll eat then head out to wherever you think we should go first. You can be my official tour guide for the day."

"Let me take a look at that map," I say, grabbing it off the table.

I fold it up and stick in my now empty Styrofoam cup.

"Hey, I need that," she says with a pout.

"No you don't. You have a Boston native as your tour guide today, remember?"

"Ah yes, it's all coming back to me now. So where do you think we should go first?"

"Don't you worry about it, I'll surprise you." I say with a sly smirk.

"Yay, I love surprises."

"Good to know."

She smiles at me as she brings her mug of coffee to her lips. I watch as she takes a sip and she doesn't take her eyes off of mine.

I don't know what it is about this girl, but damn it I want to find out.

I want to spend more time with her.

I want to know more about her.

Chapter 21

Emma

I'm excited about heading into the city with my own personal tour guide.

As much as I wanted to drive to get a feel for the streets in and out of the city, Pete insisted we take his truck. Personally, I think it's because he didn't want to be caught dead in the mini, but whatever, I'll pretend it's because he wanted to drive.

I carefully watch the street signs along the highway so that I know how to get back here when I *am* on my own.

"Are you a baseball fan?" he asks, looking over to me with those bright blue eyes.

"Well, if you're asking if I'm a Red Sox fan, the answer is yes. Just don't expect me to go all fan girl like Riley does. I'm more of a football junkie myself. Go Tarheels," I say, raising my hand in the air.

"I won't fault you for your choice in college football teams, but if you're a Red Sox fan we *have* to go to Fenway Park. Plus, there's a really good restaurant nearby the stadium we can go to lunch."

"Lunch?" I ask. "Are we making an all-day event of this date?"

"Date, is that what this is?" Pete asks, glancing over to me while scratching the stubble along his jaw line.

"Well, umm."

He starts to laugh and I feel completely embarrassed.

"I'm just playing with you, Belle," he says, giving me a subtle smirk.

"Can I tell you something, Pete?" I'm feeling a bit nervous now about the whole 'date' comment.

"Yeah, of course. You can tell me anything. That's what friends are for, right?"

"Hmm, I guess so. It's just that I'm, well, how do I say this…."

"Belle, just relax, okay? There's no pressure here with us. We're friends. We're cool. Okay?" he says, placing his hand on my shoulder.

"Okay, thanks. I haven't had a guy friend like you since college. It's just a bit weird for me, ya know?"

"It's cool, I get it. I don't have many female friends besides Char and she's more like a kid sister to me. I know where you're coming from."

I let out a heavy sigh and lean my head back on the seat. I don't know what I'm thinking—much less expecting—it's just weird to be hanging out with another guy that isn't Keith. I don't want to freak Pete out before we even get to know one another, but I don't know what I'm doing. My levels of trust with the opposite sex are pretty damn low right now. I get where he's coming from, too, it's just that I don't want to attach myself to anyone, friend or not.

I need to pull myself together. Today is supposed to be fun and relaxing. I don't want to stress out about little things.

I take in a deep breath and let it all out.

This isn't a date; it's just two people getting to know each other as friends."

I can handle that, I think.

No, I *know* I can do this. I'm stronger now than I've been in a long time. I just need to move past all the other shit I've been dealt and enjoy myself for a change.

The new Emma is going to put herself first and have a good time doing it, too.

I sit up straight and watch as Pete pulls the truck into a parking lot. He turns off the engine and moves his body to face me. I look over in his direction just as he's about to talk.

"You up for a bit of a walk?" he asks.

"Sure, where are we?"

"Well, right now we're in a parking lot."

"Funny, jackass," I laugh.

"I try," he replies with a wink. "We're near Kenmore Square; to me it's like the heart of the city. Everything we want to do is surrounding us. I don't want to overwhelm you with all of Boston in one day so I thought we'd check out Fenway, walk the square and then grab a bite to eat before heading back."

"Sounds good to me, lead the way," I say, grabbing for the door handle.

"Okay, sit tight," he says, stepping out of the truck.

I watch his figure as he walks across the front and around to my side. He opens the passenger side door and reaches his arm in for me to grab. As soon as my hand touches his there's a shock.

"Shit, lady, if you keep shocking me like that we're bound to combust soon."

"It has to be you, I haven't shocked anyone else since I've gotten here," I say, looking down at my hand.

"Well, then maybe we need to break the shock pattern," he says grabbing for my hand again. "Just fight the shock and hang on Belle, it has to give up eventually."

I hop out of his truck as he grabs onto my arm with his other hand.

"Easy, killer, big trucks aren't made for little ladies like you to hop out of; it's a big drop for you."

"Are you calling me short?"

"Nah, I'd never."

"Well good, because I was already referred to as 'old' by the guys this morning. I don't know if my ego can take another hit for being short too."

"Aww, sweet Belle, you can't be a day over thirty."

I look at him; I mean *really* look at him.

I don't know what it is, but there's something about him that pulls me to him.

It's not just a physical attraction—I'm not *near* ready for that—but the fact that he's here and getting nothing out of it has really grabbed my attention.

He's kind, sweet and someone I can see becoming a good friend.

He holds onto my hand as we walk down the side street and out into the heart of his city.

This place is amazing and there's so much going on. People are walking about all over the place. Cars are flying in and out of lanes trying to get to their destination. It's really incredible and not something I'm used to after living in North Carolina.

There are big cities down south that I've been to, but nothing that compares to this. Boston just has an atmosphere like nothing I've ever experienced before. The hustle and bustle—everyone seems to be in a rush to get somewhere.

I wonder how many people miss out on the opportunity to take in the beauty of their city.

On days like today, it's nice to just step back and appreciate what's around you. Sometimes it's best to just take a breather and enjoy the things that might not be there the next time around. I know I don't want to miss a single thing that's here for me to explore.

Being here isn't something I ever saw in my future, but I'm going to take advantage of it.

Who knew this is exactly what I needed to clear my head? Not me, but here I am, ready to take on the city of Boston with Pete.

Hand in hand, we walk down the street leading us to Fenway Park. I can see the stadium in the distance and can now understand why this is the place Riley wants to live.

I'm happy to be here.

I'm excited to start a new life in a new place.

I'm anxious for my day in the city with my new friend.

Pete

Spending today in the city with Emma has been a lot of fun.

We held hands as we walked the streets—to fight off the shock factor of course—and took a lot of pictures for her to remember this day.

Even though we were both looking forward to a quiet day on our own in the city, I can't imagine a better way to spend a relaxing Sunday than with her.

With this being her first time sightseeing in Boston, it was so cool to see her expressions as she took in all the sights of the square and Fenway Park. Once the season is back in action, we'll have to get Chloe to get us some killer seats. That is, if she's still talking to us after the breakup with Derrick.

After a much needed break from our journey, we decide to stop at Boston Beer Works for some lunch.

I got a chance to see Emma smile, laugh and try her first microbrew. She was quite the trooper, and after tasting a few beers from the selections on tap, she admitted that she isn't a beer drinker.

Note to self, Emma likes wine….not beer.

Over a few drinks—a beer for me and a glass of wine for her—Emma and I talk about her upcoming plans while staying in Boston.

This week she's in 'organization mode', as she calls it. Riley moved all of her possessions from North Carolina into a storage unit near his house. She's making a point to go through it all and bring a few things over to Derrick's house that she'll need.

Being the gentleman that I am, I offered to give her a hand if she needs it.

Since she earned a degree in project management from UNC Chapel Hill, Bryce, Char and Chloe's dad, has offered her a position with Taylor & Sons Contracting. Not only will she be the missing piece to our team's culture, but I'll also get to see her and interact with her at the office almost every day.

Once we've finished our lunch and drinks, I drive us back to the little coffee shop. As stupid as it sounds, I'm kind of bumming that this day of fun is coming to an end.

She helped to keep my mind off of a lot of things today; in fact I don't think I thought about anything but her the entire day. I'm comfortable with her and I'd like to see where this friendship goes.

Neither one of us is ready for anything more than friendship right now, but I know I want to spend more time with her.

In the two days I've known her I've laughed more than I have in months. She brings out a happier side of me that's been missing for a long time. I want to do the same for her. I don't know the whole story of what happened with her husband in North Carolina, but I want to know. I find myself wanting to know so much more about her. If nothing else we can help one another get through the struggles of our past and have fun while doing it.

I pull the truck in behind her baby blue Mini Cooper and laugh to myself.

"What's so funny?" she asks, looking ahead at her car with the cutest smirk on her face.

A piece of hair falls in front of her face as she turns toward me.

Without a thought, I reach to her and tuck it behind her ear. I let my hand linger against her face for a moment.

"Nothing, Belle," I reply, looking into her eyes.

She smiles at me. *Those eyes…damn those hazel eyes.*

"Mmhhmm. You wouldn't be making fun of the mini, would you?"

"I'd never," I reply with a smirk of my own.

"Good, because I'd hate to see our day ending badly," she says with a pout.

"So then, up 'til now you'd say it's been a pretty good day?" I ask, giving her a questionable smirk.

"Yeah, it's been a *really* good day. I had a lot of fun and I don't think I would have if I'd just gone alone."

"Me either. I'm glad I stopped here for breakfast instead of going right into the city." I give her a smile.

"Me too," she says, smiling back at me.

For a moment we just look at each other and I take her all in. As fucked up as this may sound, I don't want to let her out of the truck. I want to spend more time with her. Damn it, I want to get to know her better.

She flinches for a second and reaches into her coat pocket.

"Ugh, it's Riley again. I better get back to the house before he sends out a search party for me. Thanks so much for today, Pete, I really had a great time."

"No problem, we'll have to do it again sometime."

"Yeah, of course. Here, hand me your cell," she says, reaching her hand out to me.

I dig my cell out of my pocket and hand it over to her. I watch as she types in her number and hits save. She hands me back my phone and I look at the screen. Another smile comes to my face as I read how she entered her contact info 'Belle 326-555-1212'.

"Thanks, Belle."

"Don't be a stranger; we're friends now and I want to hang out again soon. Just give me a call and we can figure something out."

"Sounds good."

She reaches for the door handle. "Wait, sit tight," I say.

I step out of the truck and run over to her side. Opening the door, I extend my hand to help her down. She grabs onto me, and to both of our surprise, no shock.

"I think we broke the shock factor," she says, stepping onto the side walk.

"No, I think we've just gotten used to the connection we share."

I watch as her cheeks blush and she gives me a half smile looking up at me through her long lashes.

Is it weird that I don't want to say goodbye?

Is it wrong that I want to give her a hug before she goes?

Is it too soon if I want to ask to see her again tomorrow?

I don't want to come across as pushy or needy, but the past few hours have been so much fun. I've enjoyed being with her, holding her hand and listening to her tell me about what she plans to do.

There's a lot we both need to learn and understand about each other, but I know that the more time we spend together the more we'll uncover.

At this point in the game, this southern belle as piqued my interest. Whether or not we're only friends, I don't care. I knew from the moment I saw her the other day that there was something about her. I just couldn't figure out what it was. Now I think I've realized what it was about her that drew my attention.

She's sweet, caring, and after today's 'date', I've found out she's a lot of fun to be around.

There's no doubt in my mind that I want her.

I want more of Emma in my life.

Chapter 22

February 2013

Emma

The past few weeks have flown by, but I've still been able to establish a pretty good rhythm between work, the constant chaos that is Riley, Char and Derrick, and still finding time to spend with Pete.

I couldn't be happier with the way things have turned out, regardless of how scared and worried I was to come to Boston.

Things at work have been a whole different story. I'm a bit overwhelmed at the office and learning a whole new way to run the projects of the team. Thankfully, I'm surrounded by five guys that know their shit and are helping me along the way.

As for my home life, Derrick and I have fallen into a predictable routine—minus the whole sleeping in the same room and no sex—people would peg us as an old married couple.

We've found a pretty nice partnership between the two of us. Lately, his schedule doesn't get him home in time for dinner most nights; however, we both always make sure to sit down and have breakfast each morning after our run in the park.

I sit down at the kitchen table reading through a current project plan.

"Hey, Derrick. Are you going to be home for dinner tonight?" I ask while finishing up our breakfast of fruit, yogurt and coffee.

"Nah, I won't be back 'til late tonight. Trisha and I are working on two new cases with each other this week and I figure we could just get take out and eat at the firm," he says, scooping a spoonful of yogurt in his mouth.

"That's silly, Derrick, why don't you invite her over here after you're done at the office and you can eat some good home cooked food. I'm sure Trisha would rather eat my cooking than greasy take out," I say while putting my stuff in the trash and dishwasher.

"Sounds perfect. Thanks, Emma. I'll see you around seven, is that okay?"

"Yep, see you then. Have a good day, Derrick," I tell him before heading up the stairs.

Once I'm in my room, I begin to gather my clothes for work and head into the bathroom. Taking a quick shower, I fix up my hair and apply some makeup. I give myself one last glance in the mirror and head back into my bedroom to grab my briefcase and cell phone.

When I pick up my phone I see there's missed text message.

Pete – Grabbed you a coffee on the way in. Hurry up before it gets cold ☺

I smile to myself thinking of his sweet gesture. Pete and I have gotten to be pretty good friends over the past few weeks. We've gone back to the city so he could show me more of the sites, gone to a movie or two and I've schooled him on how good a southern belle can be at the game of pool.

I feel like myself again when we're together. There's no pressure of a hot and steamy romance, I don't have to worry whether or not he'll call me the next day and I can laugh again.

I shoot him a quick text back.

Belle – On my way, keep it warm for me. Be there in 15 ☺

I hurry down the stairs and out the garage door to my Mini.

The traffic is light this morning, and lucky for me, I make it over to Taylor & Sons Contracting in just ten minutes flat. I pull into my designated parking spot, grab my bag and head into the building.

I'm immediately greeted by some of the crews walking through the lobby as I make my way toward the elevator. Once inside, I push the button to the third floor and grab my phone to let Pete know I'm in the building and heading to my office.

When the elevator doors open I see him standing there holding my cup of coffee.

I shake my head and smile as I push him out of the way and walk toward my office.

"You know, the guys are getting jealous of me bringing you coffee every day," he says, grabbing my bag out of my hand so I can unlock my office door.

I push open the door and turn back to smirk at him.

"You don't bring me coffee *every* day," I say, grabbing my bag back from him.

"Actually I do, it just depends what time you get here that I give it to you or not."

"Aww Pete, you're too good to me, I'm sorry."

"Don't be, Belle. Here, take your coffee, I have to meet a crew out at a site in an hour. I'll catch you later," he says, winking at me as he walks out of my office.

I take a sip of my coffee and plop down in my comfy leather desk chair.

For the next few hours I bury myself in some upcoming projects we have planned down in Jersey.

I'm so engrossed in my work that I completely work through lunch and don't realize the time until I see Riley walking past my office.

He stops and ducks his head in.

"Hey, what are you doing moseying around?"

"I'm heading home, how late are you staying here tonight?" he asks, looking at his watch.

I glance at the clock on my wall.

"Oh shit, I had no clue what time it was. I've been sitting here since eight-thirty; I didn't even get up to pee today."

"Em, you need a life."

I scrunch my eyebrows at him, "I have a life, thank you very much."

"Well then, clean up and get out of here."

I stack the papers in a pile and shove them into my bag.

"Okay, loser, walk me to my car," I say, pushing him out of the doorway.

"So, what do you have planned for tonight?" Riley asks as we head out to the parking lot to our cars.

"Nothing too exciting. I'm making dinner for Derrick and his associate, Trisha. I told him it would be better than getting greasy take out again at the firm."

"You're a good wifey to him, Em, even though you don't get the benefits."

"I don't mind, I'm just glad we get along as well as we do."

"You'll be happy again one day, Em. You deserve that much."

I look up to my little brother and smile.

"Thanks, Riley. I'll see you later."

I hop into the Mini and drive home.

The words of my brother hit me hard and it makes me wonder if I'll ever find my true happily ever after. It might have only been a few weeks since I left Keith, but it's been months since I felt loved by him.

One day I know that I'll be happy again, but for right now I'm content. It may not be what I want or what I need, but I just know that when that person comes into my life that I won't take them for granted.

I pull up to the house and into the garage. I still have an hour or so until Derrick and Trisha get here so I decide to pour myself a glass of wine, kick off my heels and chill on the couch.

My cell phone dings, alerting me of a text message, and I reach for my phone.

I smile at the name on the screen. This man right here, he's been there for me since the first day I arrived.

Pete – thinking of you ☺

Friendship isn't always about the person you've know the longest amount of time; it's about who came into your life and never left your side.

Pete

She's on my mind morning, noon and night. I can't seem to forget about her smile and the way her eyes look up at me.

Just seeing her for a few minutes this morning has started my day off on a better note. I've never had this kind of a friendship with a female. I know that I can be myself, focus on my career and at the end of the day I still want to hear her voice.

The way we act when we're together is so comfortable. There's never a dull moment. Between our crude banter and the stories we've shared of our lives, we can talk for hours.

I don't know where this is going, but I do know that I don't want to spend a day of my life without her in it. Even if we're just friends, I'm okay with that. Well, at least I *think* I'm okay with that.

For once in my life I'm not thinking with my dick and it's crazy weird.

The sky is getting darker as I drive home. There was a time, not that long ago, that I hated to be alone in my house after Kathy left. But it doesn't bother me so much anymore. Yes, the pain of what happened is still there, but when I think about Emma all the hurt goes away.

We haven't talked about our past relationships too much, but at some point I want Emma to know how much she's helped me get through this rough patch of my life.

I pull up to my house and open the garage door.

Entering my house, I turn on the lights and hear my cell phone ring. I look at the screen and let out a heavy sigh.

"Hello, Kar," I say into the phone.

"Hey, Pete, how are you?"

"I'm good, same as I was the other day when you called to check up on me."

"You could be a little bit more appreciative of the time I take to call and check in on you," she says in a pissed off tone.

"I know, I'm sorry. Things are good. I'm doing well, work is going well and life in general is good."

"You're such a smart ass," she says with a laugh.

"I know it. So how are you and the crew?"

"We're all doing really well. The boys were asking about you the other day. Do you think you can take some time off soon and come for a visit?"

I can just imagine the sourpuss look on her face right now.

"Yeah, I'm sure I can figure out something soon. I have enough vacation time."

"Yay, the kids will be so excited!" she squeals in my ear.

"Don't say anything to them about it 'til I know when. I don't want to disappoint them like last time."

"Well, that wasn't your fault, Pete. If the bitch hadn't screwed things up you would've been here."

"I know, Kar, you don't have to remind me."

"Speaking of your love life, how are things going with your new friend Emma?"

A smile comes to my face with just the mere mention of her name. *Damn it to hell I'm developing feelings for her.*

"Kar, I told you we're just friends so there's no love life to even mention."

"I told you that you'd have a girl on your arm in a month's time. Was I right or was I right?"

"No, Kar, you're not right. It's not like that with us. Emma is a good friend and that's it. We're helping one another get through some rough times and it works for us."

"Mmhmm, have you slept with her yet?"

"Damn it, Kar, would you leave my business to me, because it's none of yours. If you want to keep prying your nose into my shit, I won't answer your calls anymore."

"You wouldn't dare," she says with a huff.

"Yeah I will if you don't cut your shit. I'm doing good and that's all you need to worry about."

"Okay fine, I'll leave well enough alone."

"Thank you. Look, I'm gonna go now. I just got home and need to grab something to eat. Tell the boys I love them and don't forget to say hi to Greg for me, too."

"I will, Pete, take care of yourself."

"Yes, *mom*," I reply sarcastically.

"We love you, Pete."

"I love you guys, too."

I hit the end button on my phone and set it down on the counter. Pulling a chair out from the table, I take a seat. My head falls between my hands and I run my fingers through my hair.

That sister of mine aggravates me to the point where I could just scream. I know she means well, but hot damn, she needs to cut this shit out.

What the fuck would she do if I told her my life sucked? No, no I don't even want to think about that because I know she'd fly her ass here in a hot minute.

I stand from the chair and walk to the fridge.

I'm starving.

I drum my fingers against the refrigerator door as I scan the shelves for something to eat. There are some leftover cabbage rolls that Emma brought me the other day. I pull out a bowel from the cabinet and fork two pieces into it. Tossing them into the microwave, I check my phone for any missed emails.

The beep of the microwave sounds off and my stomach starts to growl from the smell of the food. I pull out the bowl and set it down on the table. Sitting down, I dig into the food. *Damn the girl can cook; these cabbage rolls are delicious.*

I get up to grab my phone off the counter and touch the app to my messages. Scrolling to her name, I send her a quick text.

Pete – thinking of you ☺

I continue eating and watch the screen waiting for her to type back…pathetic, I know.

My eyes light up as her text comes through.

Belle – Oh yeah!

I laugh at her brief response. I can only imagine what she's thinking.

Pete- Yeah, I just finished eating the cabbage rolls you gave me the other day.

Belle – Yum, they were pretty tasty. I just started up some chicken chili for dinner tonight; you want me to bring you the leftovers tomorrow?

Pete – Hell yeah, you're a good cook. I'll eat anything you give me.

A few seconds go by and no text.

A few minutes go by and *still* no text.

Did she fall into the chili or am I the only loser sitting by the phone waiting for a response text?

Pete – You okay over there?

Belle- Umm, yeah I'm good.

Pete - You didn't respond so I was just checking.

Belle – Well, your last comment…You have to understand, I'm on my second glass of wine and my mind went immediately to the gutter….sorry ☹

I read her message and my message before hers; I don't get it. Her mind went to the gutter? *What the hell….ohh. Shit, how do I respond to that one?* Emma and I have never made a sexual comment to each other and now…

Yeah, she may be feeling a bit tipsy, but…shit.

Oh well, what the hell can a little harmless sexual innuendo hurt?

Pete – Watch where you let your mind wander. You never know what may happen.

Belle – umm

Pete – umm what?

Belle – I better go, I'll call you later before I go to bed

Pete – Ok ttyl

Shit, now all I can think about is Emma in bed, and me eat—…no, I can't. I get up from the table and head upstairs for a cold—*very cold*—shower.

Chapter 23

Emma

After that last text message from Pete I'm not quite sure what to think.

Pete is hot as hell with his dark, messy hair, his bright blue eyes and that sexy stubble along his jaw line.

Well actually, I know *exactly* what I'm thinking I'd like to do.

There have been so many times that I wanted to…but I didn't.

I've never made the first move with any guy, not even Keith.

Having these thoughts running through my mind, I'm getting a little hot and bothered.

I get up from the couch and walk into the kitchen to check on dinner. My mind is going a mile a minute and right now I could care less about this damn chili.

I'm not crazy to have these thoughts, am I?

Pete and I have gotten to know one another pretty well over the past few weeks. The topic of sex or anything related to sex has never come up. I just assumed he wasn't interested in me that way. For all I know, he isn't attracted to me in any way other than a friend.

I don't know all that much about what happened with his ex-girlfriend before I got to Boston. That's something that we've kind of skirted around. I want to talk to him about Keith—hell, I'm willing to tell him *everything* about me. I feel that comfortable around him.

I hear the garage door open and a few moments later I see Derrick walking in with a girl I can only assume is Trisha.

"It's smells good in here," he says, walking toward the stove.

"Get," I say, scooting him away.

I laugh at him as he moves away before I can smack him.

"Trisha, this is my wifey roommate Emma and Em, this is my associate from the firm. Trisha."

"Hi, it's nice to meet you," I say, moving forward to shake her hand.

"You too, Derrick brags you up all the time," she replies.

I look to Derrick and roll my eyes; I can only imagine what he's had to say about me.

"Can I get you a glass of wine?" I ask Trisha.

"Oh yes, please. That would be great."

I busy myself pouring Trisha some wine and finishing up dinner while Derrick runs to and from the garage, bringing boxes into the house and getting changed. Trisha and I talk about the things I've done since moving to Boston and she gives me some insight into some things that will be coming up in the next few weeks.

I'll have to check with Pete to see if he wants to tag along with me to some of the events she mentioned.

Derrick comes down the stairs and I hand him a bottle of beer.

"You're the best, Em," he says, pulling me into his side.

"Dinner should be ready in five minutes," I say.

"Sweet, thanks," he responds, letting me go and moving to the other side of the kitchen.

"So, Emma here just told me about the story of her brother and your best friend Char meeting. How crazy was that?" Trisha chimes in and takes a sip of her wine.

I have to admit that the way in which Riley and Char met was funny as hell. Only those two could live with one another and be happy.

Derrick laughs out loud and shakes his head.

"Yeah, they're something else, but I can't imagine anyone else with Charlie. Riley's perfect for her and he makes her happy. That's all that really matters," he tells Trisha.

I walk back over to the stove to check on the chicken chili. After a few stirs I decide it's ready.

I step up on my tippy toes and pull down three bowls from the cabinet.

"I made chicken chili for dinner; I hope you like things hot," I say.

I watch as Derrick looks over to Trisha and she smiles as her cheeks turn a deep shade of red.

Oh no, I hope I didn't embarrass her.

Shit, what is wrong with me and all these sexual comments? I know it's been a while for me, but geez.

The three of us sit down to eat dinner, and before I know it, Trisha and I polish off a bottle of wine.

I don't know if it was my nerves over the comment between Pete and me or the one I threw out at Trisha earlier, but the wine is going down pretty damn smooth.

The rest of the night goes off with any further sexual comments. I'm on my best behavior and we all seem to be getting along really well.

Too bad Derrick and Trisha didn't touch the box of documents they brought to the house, but at least it was a fun night.

Around eleven o'clock I say my goodbyes and head up to my room.

I'm feeling pretty damn good from the amount of wine I drank and I still have to call Pete for our nightly chat.

I strip myself of my clothes and pull on a pair of sweatpants and a hoodie. Finding a rubber band on the dresser, I pull my hair back into a ponytail.

Now if I can manage to make it into the bathroom to wash my face and brush my teeth I'll be all set.

Lucky for me I'm able to finish getting ready for bed and walk—or should I say stumble—back to my bedroom and fall into bed.

I should really close my eyes and sleep off my buzz, but I don't want to upset Pete if I don't call. I lift my head from my pillow and look around for my phone.

Shit! It's over on the dresser.

I pull myself up out of bed and walk to the other side of my room. Picking up my phone, I scroll through my recent contacts and touch Pete's name.

"Hey, Belle."

"Hey," I respond, walking back over toward my bed.

I hear him laugh through the phone.

"You doing okay over there?" he asks.

"Ugh, I think I drank a little too much wine," I say, flopping back onto my bed.

"Ohh, I see. It's not like you to drink like that during the week. Is everything okay?"

"Yeah, Derrick brought a girl from work over to the house for dinner. Before I realized it we'd drank a whole bottle of white merlot," I mumble as my face falls into my pillow.

"Derrick brought a chick over for dinner?"

"Yep, that's what he did."

"Shit, Emma, are you going to be okay? Should I call Derrick to come in and check on you? No forget that, I'm on my way, just stay where you are."

"Mmmmm, ok Pete," I slur.

I toss my phone onto the comforter and curl up in my bed, attempting to get under my covers.

Ugh, this is too much work.

Shit, I didn't feel this drunk a few minutes ago.

If I can sleep this off I'll feel so much better in the morning. Well, probably not. I'll be hung over as hell.

I snuggle into a comfortable position and close my eyes, trying to fall asleep.

Pete

As soon as I hang up with Emma, I call Derrick to let him know that I'm coming over.

He argues with me for a quick minute that he can check on her, but I insist that I want to come over myself.

I've never cared for a woman like I do for her; she's different to me in so many ways. The feelings I have for Emma are nothing like I've ever felt before.

With Kathy, I thought we were in love and that we were happy together. But now that I've met Emma, I question all the other feelings I've ever had before.

I want something from her, and although I don't know what we'll ever be, I need to be near her. Whether she needs me right now or not, I'd feel better knowing that I was there for her.

I quickly throw on a pair of sweats and a tee-shirt and head out the door to my truck.

It's the middle of the night and there's no one else on the road so I'm able make it over to Derrick's house in record time.

As soon as I pull into the driveway, I step out of the truck and head to the front door.

I turn the knob on the front door and it opens. *Thank God Derrick left it unlocked like I had asked.* I let myself into the house and start to look around for him downstairs.

I notice that the majority of the lights are out on the first floor but I see Derrick sitting in the living room watching television.

"Hey, man," I say, walking into the room toward him.

"You're crazy for driving over here. I told you on the phone you didn't have to."

"I know I didn't have to, but I wanted to."

"Dude, she's fine; I just checked on her. She's snoring away like a baby," Derrick says, getting up off the couch.

"Derrick, she's a tiny little thing and shouldn't have drank that much. When she called me she sounded wasted."

"She didn't drink any more than she usually does."

"Did she eat?" I ask with concern in my voice.

"I only saw her eat breakfast and dinner with me. I don't know if she ate anything else today. Pete, what's with you? She's fine."

"I need to check on her to make sure; I don't want anything happening to her."

"Whoa, pal. What's gotten into you?" he asks, giving me a questionable stare.

"She's my friend, Derrick. Can't I look out for my friend?"

"I don't know, dude, you've never flipped like this or came running for Chloe or Charlie."

"It's different with her, Derrick."

"Ahh I see; I think you're starting to have feelings for her," he says, punching me in the arm. "Enough of this friends shit, Pete, just admit that you care about her."

I shake my head at him.

"Look, I'm not going to stand down here and argue with you about this. It's no secret that Emma is someone special to me and I just want to make sure she's okay."

"Yeah, okay, Pete. Should I lock up down here or can you let yourself out?"

"Lock up; I'll crash on the couch tonight."

He looks at me and smiles. I push him out of my way and head up to Emma's room.

Quietly, I open the door to her room and from the light of the hallway I can see that she's passed out on her bed.

I walk into her room and shut the door behind me. I move toward her and try not to trip or make too much noise.

As I move closer, I can hear her breathing slow and deep.

Derrick was right, she's okay. I just had to see it for myself.

I sit down on the edge of her bed and she begins to move.

Sitting up in her bed, she grabs for her head.

"Hey, lay back down, Belle," I whisper.

"Pete?"

"Yeah, I'm here," I reply, reaching for her hand.

"How come? I mean, why did you come here? You drove to the house and now you're in my room?"

"You called me and I was worried so I came over to check on you."

"From your house?"

I laugh.

"Yeah, from my house. Where else would I have been?"

"I don't know, Pete, but I need to lie back down," she says, laying her head back down on pillow.

"Okay, well let me cover you back up and I'll head down to the couch."

"You don't have to do that," she says, patting the bed beside her. "Lay down here with me."

I stand at the side of her bed for a few seconds.

She has no idea how badly I want to lie down next to her, wrap her in my arms and fall asleep with her body next to mine.

"Come on, Pete, cuddle with me."

Oh dear God, it's taking all that I have not to fall into her.

"Belle, I think I should just go downstairs."

"Nope, hop in," she says, lifting the covers next to her.

Damn her. She's done something to me that no other woman has ever done; I can't say no to her.

I kick off my sneakers and pull my tee shirt up over my head, tossing it over on her desk chair.

I crawl in bed next to her, pull the sheet and comforter up around us and wrap my arm around her.

"Thanks for being a good guy, Pete," she says, scooting her body in close to mine. "I like you a lot."

A smile spreads across my face and I pull her in tight against my body.

"I like you a lot, too, Belle. Now get some rest and we'll talk about it in the morning."

"But what if you're not here when I wake up? What if this is a dream and you're not really here with me?"

"I'm here, Belle, and I promise you I'm not going anywhere without you."

"Don't hurt me, Pete," she says with a yawn. "I've been hurt too much in the past and I don't want to feel like that ever again."

"Shh, Belle, go to sleep. I won't let anyone hurt you ever again. You have me now and I'll keep you safe."

"Ok, Pete. Goodnight."

"Goodnight, my beautiful southern belle."

I close my eyes and think about every moment I've shared with this girl over the past few weeks–from the first moment I saw her until right now. I don't know what's happening between us, but I don't want it to end.

Derrick's right and I know it, too. I have feelings for this woman. I care about her and there's no point in denying that I want more than a friendship with her.

I know that we're both in a vulnerable state because of everything that we've gone through in the past, but something in me screams that I need her just as much as she needs me.

I won't let her hurt again; I only want to make her smile and be happy.

Chapter 24

May 2013

Emma

They aren't kidding when they say time flies when you're having fun.

My life has taken such a turn in the past four months and I can't believe how quickly it's gone by.

Living in a new city was the biggest change for me and I had no idea what to expect. I've been so independent for so long that having to rely on others to show me around made me feel like I was a pain in the ass.

Meeting new people was probably the biggest fear I had coming up to Boston. I knew that Riley and Char would do anything to help me out and they have; I'd be lost without them. Derrick is the other brother I'd never had, and at times really wish I didn't, but we've formed such a strong bond that I know I have a friend for life.

Pete, oh Pete. I never thought I'd meet a man like him. He's been there for me since day one. I can count on him to catch me when I fall and make me laugh when I want to cry.

We've become so close during the past few months. I didn't see it coming, but now here we are. We've agreed to take things slow and each day as it comes. It took us a while after that drunken night to talk about our feelings, but we both knew there was something special starting to happen between us.

The one thing we promised each other is that we will always communicate what we're thinking, no holding back.

He's my strength, my biggest supporter and the reason I'm happy every day. I don't know what time holds for us, but I *do* know that he'll always be a big part of my life.

Without my Boston family I wouldn't be where I am today and I'm eternally grateful for each one of them.

Today we all get to celebrate. It's a big day and I'm so excited for my little brother and Char. Riley's been a nervous wreck for weeks and hopefully after today he can calm his nerves and enjoy his future with Char.

I walk downstairs, dressed and ready to go for our morning run.

"So, are you sure about this, man?" Derrick asks, looking at Riley while he paces the living room.

"Of course I'm sure, dumbass," he replies, running his fingers through his hair.

I walk up alongside of him and wrap my arm around his waist.

"Well, if *my* opinion matters, I think you've planned a wonderful evening, little brother. Char is lucky to have you," I say in a sincere tone.

"Thanks a lot, Emma. I feel so much better now," Riley says, falling into the couch.

"I don't understand why you're so worked up about this. You two already act like a married couple. It's not like she's going to say no."

"Fuck you, Derrick. Of course she isn't going to say no. I just want tonight to be perfect for her. She means the world to me and I want this to be a night she'll remember forever. This is the kind of thing she'll tell our kids and grandkids about. I don't want to blow it."

"Look, why don't you run home, get some running gear on and head to the park with me and Emma. Maybe the fresh air and a good five miles will lift your spirits before the big night."

"Yeah, I'll be right back." Riley says and walks out the door with Manny in tow.

Derrick and I just look at each other, shrug our shoulders and start to laugh.

I feel for my little brother, I really do. He's taking a huge step forward with Char and their relationship. Even though we all know they're perfect together, I can't imagine how he must be feeling. He's planned an amazing night for her, and knowing her as well as I do, she's going to love it.

I can't wait to meet up with them later to celebrate and see her flash that diamond on her finger.

Walking into the kitchen, I bump Derrick out of my way and grab a banana out of the fruit bowel.

"Let's hope this run clears his nerves. Otherwise, I'll have to give him a Valium before they leave," I say with a laugh.

"Nah, he'll be alright. He just needs to go through with it and everything will be fine."

We walk out the front door and I wave for Riley to hurry up as he starts walking down the sidewalk.

I hop into the back seat and start eating my banana. Riley gets into the front seat and lets out a huge sigh.

"Thanks, man, this was a good idea. I need to go for a good run to get this shit out of my system."

"Don't worry, Riley, everything will go as planned. Stop stressing and have fun," I say.

"How about we make a bet," Derrick suggests.

"Last one done with the five miles buys drinks for the other two tonight," Riley says.

"Deal!" Derrick and I shout in unison.

Once we get to the park, the three of us hop out of Derrick's car and line up along the trees to stretch. Our typical route is to run through the park and meet back at the car. Now that there's a bet at stake I want to win, but I know there's no way I can out run these two clowns.

"Okay, assface, let's see if you can beat me. On your mark, get set, go!" Riley shouts as we all take off in a sprint.

As I approach the final turn leading to the parking lot, I see both guys standing next to the car drinking out of their water bottles.

Shit, piss, fuck.

"You both suck, don't even say a word," I manage to say in between breaths

Riley and Derrick look at one another and start to laugh.

Assholes.

Derrick drives up back home and drops Riley off at his house.

"Good luck tonight, Riley. We'll meet you guys out later tonight," I say.

"Thanks, Em, see you guys later."

Derrick drives down the block and pulls the car into the garage.

"What are your plans for the day?" he asks.

"I have some running around to do and then I'm meeting Pete for lunch. He was supposed to get back from his trip to see his sister in Michigan early this morning. How about you?"

"I got nothing. I think I'm just going to chill at home, maybe even take a nap later."

"Ohh wow, Derrick, you're living dangerously now," I say with a laugh.

"Yeah well, I don't get to do it often so I might as well take advantage of it."

"If I don't see you before I leave, Pete and I will pick you up before heading out to meet Riley and Char."

"Ok, sounds good."

We walk in the house together and I head upstairs to take a shower.

Pete

Anyone that enjoys flying is just nuts. The airport makes me crazy with all the people and I feel stuffed in like a sardine inside of the plane.

People are just downright rude. We all have a plane to catch, so chill the fuck out and don't try to knock me over in the process.

I hate it and can't wait to get back home to my Belle. As much as I enjoyed my visit to see my sister and her family, I'm ready to be back home in Boston with my girl.

Kar was her typical inquisitive self and asked a million and one questions about my relationship with Emma. At one point, I thought Greg was going to backslap her unless she shut her mouth. The woman is overprotective and nosy as hell, but hot damn, she doesn't need to know every intimate detail of my sex life…or lack thereof.

Although there still isn't much more to tell, since she gets updates every other day, I did let Kar know that Emma holds a special place in my heart. I'm not willing to let her go any time in the near future.

Before leaving, I gave the boys a surprise gift Emma had packed for them and told the family I'd be back again soon. I promised that the next time I came for a visit I'd make sure she was with me.

Emma truly is someone I never expected to come into my life the way she did, but now that she's here I never want to let her go. She and I have an emotional connection that I've never experienced. Every time we're together something just clicks. The sexual tension between us is out of control, but….well, that's a whole other story.

We agreed to take things slow and I can understand why—our past relationships hurt us both. But I think that we've proven to one another that we're here for each other and have no intentions of hurting the other.

It's been four months since we met and it's killing me to show her just how much she means to me. It's not that we haven't discussed it; it's just that we've never done it. When that moment happens, it's going to be intense to say the least.

We've come a long way in the past few months and she's helped me realize a few things. Yes, I love my career, my team and my crews, but without her in my life I feel like nothing is worth it. As corny and sappy as I've become since I met her, I know that we're a pair that brings out the best in each other. At least I can say that she brings out the best in *me*.

Trust is a big deal to the two of us and we've made a pact with each other to always communicate how we feel.

With Kathy, communication was something we lacked. I truly believe that if we would've talked about how we felt we could have both walked away from the relationship without hurting each other. As for Emma and her ex-husband, well he was a fucking prick that deserves to rot in hell for what he did to Emma and her family. What kind of guy can be so devious to steal what isn't his? Not only that, but he still has the nerve to come home and sleep in the same bed with the woman he's hurting?

Let's just say that if Keith ever crosses paths with Riley, Derrick or me it'll be an interesting conversation to say the least. I won't let Emma hurt like that ever again, especially if she's with me.

It's not hard to talk about my feelings with Emma; she's an open book and doesn't hold back when something bothers her. We've gotten so close that at times I feel as though I can read her thoughts just through her facial expressions.

My head snaps up and I'm pulled out of my inner thoughts as the loud speaker announces that my flight is ready to board.

I let out a heavy sigh. *Time to get back into the sardine can.*

I get in line with the other passengers as we wait to get onto the plane.

It would've been so much better if I could have taken a direct flight and returned to Boston sooner, but such is life and I guess I'll get home soon enough.

If there is any chance I can catch some rest, I'll need to try and sleep on this flight, I've got a busy ass day ahead of me and I don't want to be sleep deprived. I'm supposed to be meeting Emma for lunch and then getting together with everyone to celebrate Riley and Char's engagement.

I can't believe the putz is finally going to pop the question to the little Taylor girl.

I've seen Char grow up through the years and can see why her parents are so proud of her. I'm glad that she finally found that one person to make her happy. Riley may be a crazy loon, but he's perfect for Char. Their personalities are so similar, and even though they drive us all crazy with their public display of affection, I couldn't be happier for them.

I like our little tight knit group. Emma and I have yet to let everyone in on our little secret that we've been dating, but I don't see how they couldn't know. Well, I don't know if *dating* is the right term. We've been hanging out and spending so much time together since she got to Boston. The only thing that's really changed is that we've shared our feelings for each other.

We haven't said the whole 'I love you' bit, but I sure as hell feel as though I fell for her that night she was a drunken mess.

Listening to her southern drawl while she slurred those words to me and holding her up against my body as well fell asleep was the turning point for me. I think—no, I *know*—I was trying to keep things platonic for both of our benefits, but I can't hold back with her; she means too much to me now.

Ever since that night, I feel like I give her a piece of my heart each time we're together.

Boarding the plane, I look for my seat and toss my bag into the overhead compartment. I take my seat against the window, buckle my belt and rest my head back against the seat. If I'm lucky enough, maybe the middle seat will be left empty. Being over six foot and cramped into this tiny space is no fun, especially for a two hour flight.

I watch as the other passengers come onto the plane and find their seats. Some look as thrilled as I do about getting on board and others are smiling and laughing. I shake my head and hope that I can fall asleep, even if it's just for an hour.

A nice quick nap should help me feel more energized once we land. I close my eyes and picture holding my girl in my arms. That's exactly how I want to fall asleep every day for the rest of my life.

Chapter 25

Emma

After a morning filled with running around, I can't wait to meet up with Pete today. I'm a little over-excited to see him. It's only been a few days, but I really missed him.

I hop into my car and make my way over to his house.

My phone begins to chirp and a smile immediately comes to my face thinking it's Pete.

I hit the hands-free button without even looking at the display screen.

"Hello?"

"Emma, it's Bryce. Where are you?" he asks with panic in his voice.

"Hey, Bryce, I'm actually on my way over to Pete's house. Why, what's up?"

It's not typical for him to call me when it's not work related; he has me a bit concerned.

"Teresa and I are on our way over to Massachusetts General; Riley and Char have been in an accident."

"Oh my God, are they okay?"

My body instantly goes numb and I can barely feel my fingers on the steering wheel. I pull off the road into the nearest parking lot.

"We don't know anything yet; can you get over there as quickly as you can?"

Oh my God, this can't be good.

"Yes, I'll go back to the house and get Derrick. We'll be there as soon as we can," I say as tears begin to pool in my eyes.

"Thanks, Emma. I'll keep you posted if we hear anything before you two get there."

"Thank you."

The line disconnects and my heart sinks to my stomach. I can't pull my thoughts together fast enough.

I need to know that they're okay, that they didn't get hurt and that by the time I get there they'll be walking out the doors laughing about the whole thing.

An image of Riley and Char sitting together on the Derrick's couch flashes into my memory. They're happy, joking around and teasing me and Derrick about our living situation and the lack of sex in our lives. I'm tossing a pillow at Riley and yelling him that my sex life is none of his concern. Derrick is grabbing at Riley's head, trying to put him in a head lock, while Char is ticking his ribs.

This can't be happening. Everything was finally beginning to fall into place for our little family.

The last time I received a call like this my entire world fell apart. I've lost my parents; I can't lose my brother, too.

I need to get home and get Derrick; we need to get to the hospital as quickly as possible. Seeing that Riley and Char are okay is what I need most right now.

I make my way back home, tears streaming down my face as I say a million silent prayers that my little brother and Char will be okay.

Once I pull the car into the garage I run into the house in search of Derrick.

He's not downstairs. *Where the fuck his he?* I run up the stairs and barrel into his room.

He meets me face to face and I fall into him, crying hysterically.

"Emma, what's wrong. Why are you crying?" he asks, pushing me away from him.

"Oh my God, Derrick, hurry and get dressed; we have to go," I say in between sobs.

"Slow down, Emma. What's going on?"

"It's Char and Riley. There was an accident. We need to go to them. Now!"

"Okay, okay, Emma. Let me get dressed and we'll go," he says, searching for some clothes.

I can't concentrate on anything right now. My mind is in overdrive thinking about every possible little scrape and cut they could have. I think about how scared and worried Teresa and Bryce must feel waiting to find out what happened.

"Oh, Derrick, you have to call Chloe. Teresa and Bryce are on their way to the hospital."

I watch as Derrick attempts to throw on a tee-shirt and shorts while trying to dial Chloe's cell phone number. He places the phone between his shoulder and his ear while he waits for her to pick up. Suddenly, he tosses the phone onto his bed.

"Damn it, she's not answering!"

"You have to keep trying. She has to pick up eventually!" I yell back at him.

He looks at me for a moment; the wheels in his head are spinning.

"Go into the office and grab my briefcase. I'll Skype her," he says, digging in his closet for his sneakers.

I run out of Derrick's room and into his office. I search around the room for his briefcase, shuffle through the bag and grab the iPad.

I come back into his room and see that he's fully dressed and ready to go. He sits down on his bed and pulls up the Skype app on the iPad. I watch as he hovers his finger over her picture and finally pushes it to start the call.

Thinking that this must be hard for him to call Chloe, I place my hand on his shoulder to show support. He's been so strong since the breakup. As far as I know he hasn't even called or tried to contact her. I know it still hurts and in the back of his mind he still loves her.

Derrick has been such a huge part of my life over the past few months; I want to see him happy again. I want all of us to be happy. *Oh God, Riley and Char have to be okay.*

The line chimes a few times and finally Chloe picks up the incoming call. Her beautiful face appears on the screen and my heart starts to hurt all over again.

"Derrick," she says in a whisper.

"Chloe, I'm sorry I'm calling you like this but you didn't answer the call I made to your cell."

"Derrick, it's fine. What's wrong? Why are you upset?"

"Chloe, it's Char. She and Riley have been in an accident."

I walk away from Derrick and let him finish the conversation with Chloe. I begin to pace in the hallway as a million images of what could've happened run through my head.

Was the accident bad?

Was it just a mere fender bender?

Was it serious and are they both badly injured?

After getting off the Skype call with Chloe, Derrick finds me in the hallway and says that Chloe is getting on the next flight to Boston.

We walk back downstairs so that he can grab his keys and Derrick and I make our way over to the hospital.

On the drive over, I send Pete a text message letting him know what's going on and to be on alert for any other messages.

We pull into a spot in the ER parking lot and Derrick grabs my hand as we run toward the doors. We both scan the ER in hopes of finding Teresa and Bryce. My heart is pounding and I can't wait a second longer to find out if Riley and Char are okay.

Derrick spots Bryce and Teresa and we rush to where they're sitting. Teresa stands and wraps her arms around both me and Derrick. Bryce gives us minimal details about the accident and lets us know that Char was rushed straight into the O.R. for immediate surgery.

My stomach is in knots as Teresa cries into my shoulder. I watch as Derrick falls into the chair and the shock of what's happening hits us all hard.

Today was supposed to be one of the most important days of Riley and Char's life. Now, as we sit and wait, I'm scared that their lives may be at stake.

The four of us sit, then pace, then sit while we wait to hear any updates from a doctor.

Time goes by and we still don't know the status of either family member.

I'm beginning to feel sick.

Derrick's parents, Rose and Bud, show up and again we still haven't received an update.

Two hours have gone by and the six of us are still waiting. The anxiety starts getting to me and I need to go for a walk. I let Derrick know that I'm going to the cafeteria for some coffee and to call me if anyone comes to talk to them. Rose offers to go with me, and after a lot of persuasion on everyone's part, Teresa decides to go along with us.

The three of us walk arm in arm to the cafeteria.

"I can't believe this is happening," Teresa cries.

"I know," I say, pulling her into my side.

"Emma, you must be frantic," Rose says.

"I'm praying they're okay. I just don't understand why it's taking so long for someone to come down and talk to us."

"It's ridiculous if you ask me," Teresa says.

"All we can do it sit and wait, it's not fair," I reply.

"Has anyone heard from Chloe?" Rose asks.

"Derrick's been communicating back in forth with her. She's on a plane right now."

"I wish she was here right now," Teresa says.

"Soon we'll all be together to help support and pray for Riley and Char," I tell her.

As much as I want to cry and curl up in a corner, I have to be strong for Teresa and Derrick until Chloe gets here.

The three of us each grab two coffees and head back to the ER waiting room. Just as we round the corner I hear Derrick yelling.

"This is fucking ridiculous! Someone has to tell us more. They could both be dead right now for all we know," he says as we all watch him punch the chair next to him.

"Derrick Mason Peters, don't talk like that!" his mom shouts.

"Damn it, Mom, someone has to know something. This isn't right. What if one of them needs us? We can't help them from out here."

I walk over next to him and hand him a cup of coffee.

"Here, take this and let's go walk outside," I say, gesturing my head toward the doors.

He looks up at me with his blue eyes rimmed in red, pauses for a moment and then gets up to walk outside with me.

"Some fresh air may help to clear our minds," I say as my cell phone begins to vibrate in my pocket.

We make our way outside and over to a concrete wall.

"Yeah, I guess so," he replies taking a seat.

I pull out my phone. It's Pete looking for an update.

Pete – any news?

Belle – no, still waiting ☹

Pete – I'll be there soon, Belle. I'm meeting the guys and then picking up Chloe from the airport. LMK if you hear anything else.

Belle – I will xoxoxo

Derrick and I sit out on the curb for what feels like forever, drinking our coffees, until we see Bryce coming out to get us.

"We just spoke to the doctor that saw Riley and Char when the ambulance brought them into the ER."

"Thank fuck, it's about time. What did they say?" Derrick says.

"Well the good news is that Riley's okay. He has a broken humerus, collar bone and a few cuts from the windshield breaking, but we can go see him in a few minutes."

I let out a heavy sigh. *What a relief.*

"Okay, so if that's the good news, what did they say about Charlie?" Derrick asks.

Bryce's face floods with tears.

"She's still in surgery. She's broken the majority of her bones on the right side and has a severe head injury. Even after surgery it will be difficult to know what will happen for a few days. She needs to wake up and come back to us. Then we can help her heal with the rest of her injuries."

Tears fall from my eyes as Derrick grabs onto me and Bryce.

The three of us walk back through the door and into the ER to sit with our families.

Chapter 26

Emma

We wait…and we wait…and we wait some more.

I've always thought I was a patient person. That is, until today.

How is it possible that a place filled with doctors and nurses can take so long to let us in to see a patient?

After about another hour's wait, an ER doctor comes out to let us know we can go in to see Riley.

Right now he's limited to only two family members per visit so Teresa and I volunteer to go in first.

Even though I know Riley has limited injuries, I'm still nervous to go in and see him.

The doctor escorts us through the doors and toward Riley's room.

My stomach feels sick and my heart is beating a mile a minute. It's been a long day of sitting and waiting. We finally have our answers about Riley, but there's still the looming concern of what's happening to Char in surgery.

Teresa tells me to go into the room first. I'm scared and don't know what to expect.

When I walk into the room, Riley is sleeping. He's propped up with pillows in a hospital bed wearing a light blue Massachusetts General Hospital gown. His head is wrapped in a white bandage and random pieces of his brown hair are coming out the top.

As I move in closer, I can see that he hasn't been cleaned up yet. He still has dried blood on his face, neck and chest. His arm is in a crazy looking cast contraption. *How the hell can he be sleeping in that position?*

Teresa and I look at one another and shake our heads. I want to talk to him, but I know I shouldn't wake him up.

I pull over two chairs next to his bed so that Teresa and I can sit. After a few moments a nurse comes in to check his vitals and he begins to wake up. I stand up next to him and grab his hand.

 "Emma," he mumbles.

"Hey Riley, don't try to move or talk. Just take it easy."

He begins to shake his head.

"Where's Char? Where's my girl?" he asks, trying to sit up.

"Riley, don't. You need to lie back and rest," I tell him while trying to push him back down onto his pillows.

"This is all my fault. I should've been able to help her. I need to see her."

"Riley, none of this is your fault. There was nothing you could've done to prevent this accident. We need you to chill and lay back down. If you're not well enough they won't release you. What good will you be to Char if you can't help her get better?"

The nurse finishes up his vitals and changes his IV bag. She tells us that they're going to take him up for a CT scan and he should be back in about an hour.

I lean into my brother and give him a half hug and a kiss on the forehead.

"You had me worried, little brother. Listen to the nurses and doctors and I'll be back in to see you in a bit," I say as the tears fall from my face.

He lays back down on the pillows and gives me a smirk.

"Come back with some good news about Char. I want to see her and tell her I love her."

I give him a smile and turn to follow Teresa out of the room.

As we walk back out to the waiting room, Bryce and Derrick stand and walk toward us.

"How is he?" Derrick asks.

"He looks like shit and it seems like he's in a lot of pain," I reply.

"He's really beating himself up over this, Derrick. You need to go in there and tell him this isn't his fault. He was knocked out with the impact and feels he should've been able to protect Char," Teresa says as the tears fall from her cheeks.

I pull Derrick to the side while Bryce comforts Teresa.

"Derrick, I know you and Riley are close, but I know him better. Teresa wasn't joking when she said he's taking this hard. Char is his whole world. I've never seen him care about anyone as much as he does her. We need to keep him focused on getting himself better and not about her. I know it's a lot to ask, but can you do that for him? Help him not think about her?"

"Emma, do you realize what you're asking me to do? Those two have been attached at the hip since the moment they met. They have a magnetic pull, and without each other, they are a fucking mess. How do you suppose I help him not think about her?"

"I don't know, Derrick, but I *do* know my brother. If he has *his* way he'll unhook every cord attached to him and march his way up to the ICU."

"I can't promise you anything, Emma, but I'll stay by his side. Are you going to go stick around and go back in with me later?"

"No, I'm going to run home. I need to shower and change. Do you want me to bring you anything?"

"Nah, I'm good. Thanks, Emma. My parents just left to go get something to eat. I'll see you guys when you get back."

I walk back over to the chairs and pick up my things. Before I leave I give a hug to both Bryce and Teresa. While walking toward the doors I pass Derrick, pat him on the shoulder and mouth, *thank you.*

I hop into Derrick's car and make my way back to the house.

I can't be thankful enough to know that my brother is okay. I don't know what I would've done if something were to ever happen to him. He's the only family I have left and I can't lose that—I can't lose *him*.

As I pull onto our street I decide to drive up to Riley and Char's house to check on the pooch.

Poor Manny has been stuck inside all day. I let him outside to run around for a few minutes while I fill his food and water bowls and make sure the doggy door is open. At least this way he can let himself in and out until I come back later tonight.

I whistle for Manny to come back inside. Once he starts to eat, I walk out the front door and make my way back down to Derrick's house.

I don't want to stay away from the hospital for too long so I quickly jump into the shower, change and grab some things for us all to eat before heading back.

Pete

My nerves are a wreck and I'm tired as hell.

I haven't spoken to Emma, except through text message, and I want so badly to be by her side at the hospital. I want to help this family that's such a huge part of my life.

After texting with Derrick, the only thing I knew I could to do to be of any help was to pick up Chloe from the airport.

Bryce had kept me, Chris and Tony up to date with any news throughout the day. Now that we're about to get Chloe and head to the hospital, I just want to comfort my girl and let her know how much I really do care about her.

Times like this really put things into perspective for a person. Emma means the world to me and in a short time she has shown me what it means to truly love another person.

An accident took her parents away from her over a year ago and I can only imagine the pain and grief she's feeling right now.

I park the truck in short term parking and the three of us walk into the airport to find Chloe.

As we stand at the gate, I watch as all the passengers are greeted by their loved ones. Once Chloe comes out I don't know what kind of reaction she'll have. She just flew cross country to be with her sister, who we still don't know will be alright or not.

She exits the tunnel and my eyes immediately find hers as I start to walk her way.

I pull her into my side, no words said, but the emotions are evident.

We insist that she sit up front and Chris takes her suitcase, tossing it into the back of the truck, while Tony opens the passenger side door for her.

The ride to the hospital is made in complete silence; no one is willing to utter a word.

I watch Chloe through the corner of my eye and can see that she's tensing up the closer we get to the hospital. I look over in her direction and grab onto her hand to show my support. I want to reassure her that everything will be okay. I want to make it okay. I don't know how, but I'll do whatever I can to help her.

She looks over in my direction and gives me a slight smile.

We pull into Massachusetts General Hospital's parking lot and I release a heavy sigh.

I turn off the truck and look over to Chloe. She looks scared, anxious and like she's about to be sick.

"Chloe, are you okay to get out and walk to the door? You look like you're about to pass out," I ask.

I can see that her entire body is trembling.

The guys and I get out of the truck, open her door and stand outside until she's ready.

"We'll walk right in with you, sugar," Tony says.

"Yeah, I'll even hold your hand if it'll make you feel better," Chris tells her.

I watch as she reaches for Chris's hand and steps down out of the truck. I wait until she moves away to close the door and then grab onto her left hand.

As soon as we enter the hospital, Tony heads over to the information desk to find out where we need to go. Chris and I still have a hold of Chloe's hands. I don't want to let her go until I know she's good and ready to do this on her own.

Tony comes walking back over to us and glances down at our hands connected to hers.

"You would think these two douche bags were your only life line, Chloe," Tony says with a smirk.

"Well, if this is the lifeline I need to survive, I think I'll just deal," she tells him while looking back in forth between me and Chris.

I look down into her big brown eyes as I squeeze her hand, "You ready to do this, doll?"

"As much as I would like to say no, I think we better get up there. Lead the way, Tony," she says, lifting her arms to get me and Chris moving.

The four of us walk into the elevator and Chris hits the button to the fourth floor.

As the doors open we can see the visitors' waiting area off to the right. We walk off the elevator, around the corner and through a set of wooden doors. My eyes immediately fall on Emma's and my heart falls to my stomach.

I can see the pain in her eyes and I want to rush over to her and erase the pain she's going through.

She's sitting next to Derrick and surrounded by the rest of their families.

I glance down at Chloe; she's breathing a bit heavier than she was before and looks white as a ghost. I don't know if the fact that Char was in an accident just hit her or if it's that she just locked eyes with Derrick, but she's about to freak out.

"Hey, you okay Chloe?" I ask.

She shakes her head no and I feel like I need to help her calm down. I lead her back out of the waiting area and toward the restrooms down the hall. I open the door, nod my head for her to go in and follow right behind her. Walking over to the sinks, I grab for a paper towel and splash some water onto it.

"Here, take this and wipe your face. You need to calm your breathing down before you have a panic attack. And believe me, I've been on drugs for years for those fuckers."

She looks at me with a blank expression and takes the towel from my hand.

"I know you're freaked out about Char, but she'll be fine. You two girls are the biggest fighters in Boston; you can get through anything," I tell her, giving her a smile.

"Pete, it's not that. I mean, it's not Char. Well, yeah I'm a nut case with everything that happened today, but seeing Derrick here with his girlfriend. Damn it, why did he have to bring her here. Was she close with Char? Is that why she's here?"

I give her a look. *What the fuck is she talking about? Derrick doesn't have a girlfriend.*

"Chloe, what the hell are you talking about? Of all people, I should know if Derrick has a girlfriend, and he doesn't. Who are you talking about? The only girls out there are your mom, his mom and Emma. And *she* sure as hell isn't Derrick's."

She looks down at the floor, back up at me and then back to the floor.

"I've been so consumed about Char that I totally forgot about Riley. Emma is Riley's sister and I...I thought she was with Derrick. I mean, when we walked in there, I saw...well, they were holding hands and...ugh, I'm a stupid idiot."

I grab the shredded paper towel from her hands and toss it into the trash. I need to get her attention. I lift her chin with my fingers, forcing her to look straight into my eyes.

"Look, Chloe, I've known Derrick as long as I've known you. The two of you are perfect for one another. Just get your shit worked out, because honestly, I'm sick of hearing him bitch like a girl about you. He loves you and you love him. Deal with it and make it work. Capiche?"

She laughs and nods her head up and down.

"Capiche," she responds.

"Okay then, get yourself cleaned up and meet us back out in the waiting room."

I walk out of the ladies' restroom and back to the waiting area to find my girl.

Chapter 27

Emma

My eyes light up as I see Pete walk back into the room. He comes down to sit next to me and I lean into him as he grabs for my hand. At this point, I could care less if they all figure out we're together. It's going to come out sooner or later and right now I need him the most.

"You doing okay, Belle?"

I look at him and stare into his blue eyes.

"I'm just so glad you're here now."

"Me, too. I wish I could've been here the whole time with you. I'm so sorry; I can't imagine how you must've been feeling,"

"It's okay. You got Chloe here and that's what we needed. Thank you."

"Have you guys heard anything new about Riley and Char?" he asks.

I shake my head, "No, nothing new. We're just waiting to see what happens with Char and hopefully Riley will be released soon. He's really beating himself up over the accident. I tried to tell him that it wasn't his fault, but he's so protective of Char."

"I know, I'd feel the same way if it were you," he says, leaning in to kiss my forehead.

"Really?"

"Really," he says. "I don't know what I'd do if anything ever happened to you."

I give him a smile and rest my head on his arm.

I watch and listen to the conversations surrounding us. There is so much tension and anxiety flowing through this room it's almost too much to bear.

"Hey, you wanna go for a walk? I need to get outta here for a little bit."

"Yeah, sure."

"Okay, let me text Derrick and see if he wants to get away for a bit with Chloe. I think those two need some time alone to talk; they're beginning to make me antsy."

Pete laughs and nods his head.

I pull out my phone and send a text to Derrick.

Emma – Let's go for a walk and grab some coffee....oh yeah, and bring that cute brunette before Pete snags her ;)

I watch as Derrick digs into his pocket for his phone. He looks up at me, shakes his head and gives me a smile.

Pete stands from his chair and moves in front of me. We walk over to Derrick and wait for him to ask Chloe to come with us. I watch as he extends his hand to her and she accepts. I almost feel giddy for these two.

It's not hard to see that they still have strong feelings for one another. I've never even met the girl and I can tell that she's still madly in love with him. A little time alone for these two and I guarantee they'll work things out.

Chloe lets her parents know that we're going for a walk and to let one of us know if they hear anything. We walk out of the waiting area and out toward the elevator.

"So, where we going?" Chloe asks.

"Well, Pete and I are going for a walk outside to get some fresh air," I say. "And we both agreed that you and Derrick need a chance to talk. The sexual tension is thick enough to get your *parents* in the mood for a little wam-bam-thank-ya-ma'am up there."

"Fuck, Emma, that's just gross," Derrick says. "But I *do* agree that we should talk. You wanna go to the cafeteria and grab some coffee?"

"Yeah," Chloe replies.

The four of us get onto the elevator, but Pete and I stay on while Derrick and Chloe get off on the second floor.

"You think those two will be okay?" Pete asks.

"Yeah, they need time to talk and there's no way they can do that with both of their parents sitting in the same room."

"I agree. Good thinking, Belle."

"Thanks. Seeing them together, I can tell that they still love each other. They just need to talk some things through and see if their love is strong enough to make it work again."

The elevator doors open to the first floor and Pete leads me out of the lobby and to the front of the hospital.

There's a concrete wall off to the side that he leads us to. He hops onto the wall and pulls me in between his legs.

It's already gotten dark outside and there's a warm breeze flowing through the air.

My hair whips across my face and Pete pulls it away, tucking it behind my ear.

I wrap my arms around his waist and rest my head on his chest.

"You know, I really missed you the past few days. It's the first time we've been apart since you moved up here," he says.

I pull away from him just enough that I can look up into his eyes.

"I missed you, too. I mean, it was nice to talk to you on the phone, but it wasn't the same as you being here with me."

"I told Kar the next time I come for a visit I want you to come with me."

"Really? You'd want me to meet your family?"

He lets out a laugh and gives me a smirk.

"Yeah, why wouldn't I want to you meet them?"

"I don't know. We've kept *us* a secret from everyone all this time. It's just….I don't know. I guess it just means a lot for you to want me to meet them."

"Belle, you're a part of my life now and I want everyone to know it. Today really put a lot of things into perspective for me and I know now more than ever that I don't want to lose you. I don't know what I'd do if anything ever happened to you, Emma. You've captured my heart and I'll never let you go."

We've never said 'I love you' to each other, but that sure as hell felt like it to me.

"I feel the same way about you, Pete. You came into my life when I needed a friend. You were there for me to fight through one of the biggest struggles of my life. You're a part of my life that I'll never let go."

I stand up on my tip toes and press my lips to his.

A shock runs through my body, but nothing like it used to. Pete's tongue licks my bottom lip and I open my mouth for him to explore mine. Kissing him is like nothing I've ever experienced. He's gentle, loving and passionate. He pulls me in closer to him and I realize that I've fallen in love with him. Not a day goes by that I regret the decision to move here. If I hadn't, I never would've met the man that I know will give me my happily ever after.

Slowly, we pull away from one another and he kisses me on my lips, my nose and my forehead.

"As much as I'd love to stay out here and kiss you all night, we should go back in and see how the love birds are doing."

"Sounds good, Belle."

He hops down off the wall and wraps his arm around me, pulling me close to him.

We make our way back into the hospital and head up to the cafeteria.

When we walk inside, I see Derrick and Chloe kissing and a smile comes across my face. I look up at Pete and he's smiling, too.

"So, did you guys talk or just make out the whole time?" Pete asks.

"Shut up, asshole! Chloe just gave me some incredible news. She's coming back to Boston to work strictly with the Red Sox. She's going to be the Senior Analyst for the team. Isn't that incredible?"

"That's great, Chloe! Congrats!" I say. "Does that mean I need to find a new place to live?"

"Oh God no, Emma! You're always welcome at my...I mean, our house. Right, Chloe?" Derrick says, looking back at Chloe.

"You know what? This is all happening so fast. But, Emma, I'll say that if Derrick wants you to stay then you stay. I really haven't even considered where I'd be living."

"What are you talking about, Angel? You'll live in our house," he says in a sincere tone.

"Okay, Derrick, let's just step back for a second, okay? I still need to get through my final interview and then move all my shit back home. Let's take it one day at a time, okay?"

"Whatever you say, Angel, you just made me the happiest guy in all of Boston. I have my girl with me and knowing that you could be coming back home is enough for me. At least for right now."

"Fair enough," she says and kisses him on the lips.

"Well, if you two lovebirds can keep it in your pants for a few more hours, why don't we go up and check on Char and Riley?" Pete says.

"Yeah, by now we should be good to go up and see Charlie," Derrick says.

Pete and I lead the way back to the elevator.

I'm so happy for Derrick; he's such a great guy and deserves to be just as happy as I am, if not more.

The four of us pile back into the elevator and I can't help but smile up at Pete as Derrick wraps his arms around his girl.

Together we get off the elevator and I watch as Derrick and Chloe walk hand in hand in front of us toward the visiting area.

As soon as we walk in, all eyes focus on the happy couple. In no time at all Derrick opens his mouth about Chloe's possible move. For a brief moment, everyone's attention is on them and not the reason why we're all here. It's nice to see everyone smiling and happy again.

After the biggest group hug ever, Derrick and Chloe decide to go in and see Riley.

Pete and I take a seat with everyone else and wait until we get word on Char.

Pete

Looking around this room, I'm overwhelmed by the support and love for Riley and Char. I know the waiting is starting to get to everyone, but there's not too much we can really do about it.

I wrap my arm around Emma and pull her in close to my side. I love having her here with me right now. I've missed seeing her—touching her—and now all I want to do is love her. I don't know what the future holds for us, but I do know that I want her to be a part of mine.

Our brief talk outside told me that we feel strongly for one another, but I still don't know where that leaves us.

I know that now is not the right time or place for us to decide where our relationship should go, but at some point soon, I know that we need to sit down and talk about it.

The news of Chloe possibly moving back to Boston is incredible for her and Derrick, but it makes me wonder what Emma will do.

Will she stay in Derrick and Chloe's house?

Will she move out and get a house or apartment of her own?

Will she…would she move in with me if I asked her?

There really is so much we need to talk about and I don't want to push her into anything too soon. The last thing I want to do is hurt her or scare her because I'm moving too fast.

It drives me crazy how much I care about her. I watch as she talks with everyone. Her smile and those eyes can light up a room, at least for me they can. She's such a caring person; always putting the needs of others before her own.

I know one of the things she wanted to accomplish with her move to Boston was to start putting herself first more often. It's hard for her; it's not in her nature to push others away. It's one of her qualities that makes me love her so much. No matter what she needs or what I want to do for her, she always makes a point to make sure I have what I need first.

She's something so special to me now that I don't know what I would do if I lost her.

The doctor comes into the room and all eyes move toward him as he walks over to Bryce.

Both Teresa and Bryce stand and walk toward the far left corner of the room. The entire room goes silent and Emma pulls away and moves over to sit next to Derrick's mom.

I instantly miss the loss of her body next to mine.

I look around the room at the expressions on everyone's faces.

I'm not a parent. I have no children, and I don't know if I ever will, but to see the pain in these parents' faces kills me.

Bryce is one of the toughest guys I know and I've seen him cry over the fear of his daughter's wellbeing. Watching as the doctor talks to them, I see he's trying to comfort his wife. She has her body pressed firmly against him while he runs his hand up and down her back.

Riley, Derrick and Chloe come back into the room and Riley immediately walks over to where the doctor is talking to Char's parents. He steps in alongside of Teresa and she swings an arm around his waist.

After what feels like an eternity, the doctor walks out of the room. Bryce, Teresa and Riley walk over to the rest of us and take a seat in the row of chairs directly across from where Emma, Rose and Bud are sitting.

I watch as everyone sits in silence. Bryce's leg is bouncing, Teresa is twirling her wedding ring and Riley is drumming his fingers on the arm of his char.

"Will someone please say something?" Chloe says, fidgeting in her chair.

Riley's head snaps up and looks toward Char's mom.

"Of course, honey. I think I'm just in a bit of shock." Teresa says, holding onto Bryce with one arm and Riley with the other.

This isn't even my sister, girlfriend or immediate family member and the suspense is killing me to find out how she's doing.

Riley looks around the room and finally speaks.

"Well, she won't be coming home anytime soon, but they're happy with her progress. She's responded to a lot of the tests they've been doing on her, which is good because it shows normal brain activity. They also just took her off the respirator and she's breathing on her own again."

Riley pauses for a moment and runs his hands through his hair.

"Why the fuck didn't you tell me she was this bad?" he asks, looking between Derrick and Emma.

Emma's mouth drops open and I can tell she's taken aback by his reaction.

"Riley, we couldn't have you going crazy while you were under care, too. Don't be mad at us. You're up to date now and know that she'll be fine," she says.

"That's my girl up there. I would've liked to know what was happening. God, what if something worse would've happened? I wouldn't have been able to live with myself," he says frantically.

Riley pushes off of his chair and starts to pace behind the row of chairs. He sticks his hand in his pocket and pulls out the ring box. Holding it in his hand, he grips it tightly and puts his hand over his heart.

"Riley, what is that in your hand?" Chloe asks, standing from her chair and walking toward him.

He looks up at her with tears in his eyes.

"It's your sister's engagement ring. I was going to propose to her tonight."

"Oh my God, Riley," she says, her hand flying to cover her mouth.

The pain I see in my friend's expression is unbearable. He loves Char with his entire being and now he's unsure what will happen to her, to him and to their future.

Chapter 28

Emma

The sunlight shines in through the blinds of the sliding glass doors in the living room. I feel the warmth on my face and the strong arms that are wrapped around my body. I scoot myself back against him so that my entire body is flush against his.

He begins to stir and a smile comes to my face.

After the long day and night at the hospital, I offered to come back to Riley and Char's house. For one, I wanted Manny to have some company and two, I wanted Derrick and Chloe to have some time to spend alone.

When Pete suggested that he'd come stay with me there was no way I was going to say no. Since he'd been gone all week, I was over the moon excited that I'd get to spend some one on one time with him.

Yesterday was a difficult day for all of us; it's going to be even harder until we know exactly how Char will progress once she wakes up.

Pete was right, an accident like that can really put things into perspective for a person. Between him being away for the past few days and the scare we all had yesterday, I know that I don't want to lose this man. He's become a constant in my life and without him I don't know how well I would've gotten through the past few months.

I enjoy his company not just as a friend anymore. I realized yesterday that I want more from him, from us. After what he told me, I know now more than ever that we both share strong feelings for one another. Now we just need to decide what we want to do about it.

He squeezes his arms around me just as Manny comes over to the couch to give me a good morning kiss across my face.

"Eww Manny, get away!" I screech, pushing his face away from mine.

Pete laughs in my hair and I nudge him in the stomach with my elbow.

"Ouch! Hey, watch where you stick that little elbow of yours."

"Not funny, Pete, that was gross. My face is now covered in dog drool," I say, trying to pry my arms free from Pete's grasp.

"Sorry, Belle, but I can't blame him for wanting a kiss from you first thing in the morning."

"You're cute, Pete, but no kisses from this gal until I get to brush my teeth."

He moves his arms from me and pushes me off of the couch. I fall to the hardwood floor and immediately have Manny all up in my business.

"Ugh, Manny, back up for a second. Nothing like getting kicked out of bed and slobbered on by a dog first thing in the morning."

I look up to Pete who is now laughing into a pillow.

"You two both suck, you know that, right?" I say, getting up off the floor.

Pete moves the pillow from his face, his blue eyes staring back at me and a pout on his face.

"Don't try that with me, buddy. You're the one that just pushed me off the couch."

He sticks out his bottom lip. "Sorry, Belle, come here and I'll make it up to you."

I shake my head no and hit him in the head with a pillow.

"Nope, sorry, too late now," I say, giving him a smirk.

I walk toward the kitchen and Manny follows close behind.

"Alright, boy, let's get you fed and outside for a bit. Aunti Em has to go back to the hospital today to visit your mommy and daddy."

I bend down and rub behind his ears.

"Don't worry, they'll be back home soon," I say as he falls to the floor and rolls onto his back.

I rub his belly for a few moments and can sense Pete standing behind us.

"Belle, you're too cute. You *do* realize you're talking to a dog?"

I look up at him and squint my eyes to give him a glare.

"Yes I do, but Manny is more than a dog to us. He's Riley's right hand man; has been for years. He's a part of the family."

"I know, Belle, I was just playing with you," he says, walking toward the kitchen door.

I watch as he opens the doggy door and snaps his fingers. Manny rolls back onto his belly and jumps up to head outside.

Pete grabs my hand to help me up off the floor and leads me to the kitchen sink. He pulls from behind his back the toothbrush and toothpaste I'd packed from home.

He starts to run the water in the sink and squeezes some paste onto the brush.

I look at him and he just smiles.

He puts the brush into his mouth and starts to swish the toothpaste around, cleaning each one of his teeth. He leans over the sink and spits. Handing me the toothpaste and brush, he cups his hands under the water and brings it to his mouth. I watch him as he rinses the remaining toothpaste from his teeth and makes one last spit into the sink.

Holy hell, who knew watching a man brush his teeth could be so hot?

"Now your turn, sweet Belle."

He takes the toothpaste and brush back from my hands. I stand in complete silence and stillness as he squeezes more paste onto my toothbrush. He sets the tube down on the counter and ducks his head down to be level with me.

"Open up, little girl," he says as his cool minty breath hits me in the face.

I open my mouth and he sticks the toothbrush in to start cleaning my teeth.

I tilt my head up so that he can see what he's doing. I stare into his eyes as his tongue darts out of his mouth. He's paying close attention to care for every inch of me.

He gently slides the brush in and out of my mouth, making sure that every tooth is thoroughly clean.

"Okay, good to go…now spit," he says, running my toothbrush under the running water.

I spit the toothpaste out of my mouth and take the cup of water he just filled for me. I rinse, spit and repeat until I feel that the last of the toothpaste is out of my mouth.

Setting the cup down on the counter, I turn to him and wrap my arms around his waist.

"Thank you," I say, looking up at him.

"You're welcome, Belle."

"I can't say that anyone, other than me and my dentist, has ever brushed my teeth," I say with a giggle.

He picks me up in his arms and turns me to sit down on the counter top. I wrap my arms around his neck and pull him closer to me.

"Belle, I want to do so many things to you, for you and with you. I want to make you as happy as you've made me these past few months. Whether it's brushing your teeth, walking you through Boston or just sitting at home holding you in my arms, I want you to be by my side."

My heart skips a beat with the words he's saying to me.

I can't fight it any longer. *I love him.*

Pete

I watch her facial expression closely as she takes in the words I'm saying to her. Her hazel eyes are shining back at me, her lips are curved up in a smile and a slight blush is tinted on her cheeks. She really is a beautiful woman and she's my little southern belle.

I so badly want to be a bigger part of her world; I want to *be* her world.

I know that we're already together nearly every day, but that's not enough for me anymore; there's so much more from her that I want.

She's changed the way I view life. I've concentrated so much on me the past few years that I never paid close attention to my personal happiness. She's shown me that I deserve to be happy and I want to do the same for her.

Since the breakup with Kathy, I thought I'd never find someone that would love me for *me*. Someone that would forgive me for my flaws and enjoy the things I'm able to offer. Someone that would not only be my partner but would also be my best friend. I realize now that I want someone to be with me forever.

Emma is the one I want to spend every day with for the rest of my life. I want to grow old with her and give her everything she's ever wanted. I want to keep her safe and make sure that no one is ever able to hurt her again. I want to give her the world and show her there's more to us than just a friendship.

She's made me fall for her with everything that she is—her smile, her laugh and the way she looks at me.

I just can't get enough of her and I want to make her mine for good.

She leans into me so that our faces are mere inches apart.

I can feel her breath against my face and I can't wait a second longer to kiss her again. I close my eyes and my mouth finds hers. She bites down on my lower lip and I slide my tongue into her mouth. Her hands move into my hair and I begin to caress her back.

This kiss is different from the last; it's harder, deeper and more urgent. There's a need that we're both trying to fulfill. At this point, I want nothing more than to strip her naked on this counter and kiss, touch and love every inch of her body.

While my tongue strokes hers she lets out a moan, and instantly there's a slight discomfort pushing against the zipper of my jeans. I don't know that I have the willpower to wait much longer; I need to be inside of her.

"Belle," I pant, breaking free of our kiss.

"Yes," she replies, looking into my eyes.

"I need you," I say as I begin to kiss her lips, her jaw and her neck.

"Yes," she replies, pulling my face back up to hers.

I look into her hazel eyes and the feelings I have for her are ready to burst through me. If I could shout to the world how much I love this girl I would.

"I need you to know how much you mean to me, Belle," I say while peppering kisses all over her face.

"I already know, Pete."

She pulls me back into her and wraps her legs around my waist. Her body is tight up against mine and she has to notice that my erection is now pushing against her.

I lift her up off the counter and carry her into the living room. Laying her down on the couch, I prop myself up with one arm and hover over her body.

My lips immediately find hers and I deepen the kiss. Our lips lock, our tongues twisting together and our bodies craving to be united as one.

She bucks her hips up against mine and at any moment I feel like I'll explode…either that or someone is going to walk in on us.

I feel like a fucking teenager about to dry hump his girlfriend in her parents' basement. This situation is somewhat different but fuck, I don't want to do this with her here.

For a moment I break our kiss and look down at her.

She shifts her tiny body underneath me and I can't—*I won't*—do this with her on her brother's couch.

I don't want her to think I don't want her.

She starts to nip at my neck and I feel as though I am about to go crazy. God, I don't want her to stop. But I do. She has to stop, *we* have to stop.

"Belle, I want you, but I want you in my bed. I want our memories to be something we can share forever. When I lay my head down, I want to remember that my bed was the place we made love for the first time. I want to remember you, all of you," I say and then pause a moment. "Plus, this damn dog won't stop staring at us. Look at him. He's drooling."

Emma turns her head and looks next to the couch, and sure enough, Manny is sitting there watching us with his tail wagging.

She starts to laugh and covers her face with her hands.

"Damn it, Pete. Your level of self-control is beyond anything I could ever imagine; I don't know how you do it. I've wanted you for so long, and now we wait again," she says with a pout on her beautiful face.

"Don't worry, Belle. When our time is right, it will be worth the wait."

She smiles up at me and I lean down to kiss her on the lips.

Yes, I want to savor this woman.

Yes, I'm dying inside to be with her in the most intimate way.

Yes, I hate that we have to wait for another time.

When that moment happens for us it's going to be the first time I make love to my girl and the last time I ever tell a woman that she's stolen my heart.

I love Emma and there's no one else that I'll ever want to spend my life with like I do with her.

Chapter 29

Emma

Holy fucking hell. My panties are drenched, my heart is pounding out of my chest and the thoughts running through my mind are starting to cloud my reality. If the sexual tension between me and Pete gets any more intense I'm likely to combust right in front of him.

I let out a heavy sigh as he gets off of me and moves to sit at the end of the couch. I watch him through hooded eyes and there is nothing I want more than to strip him naked and ride him off into the sunset.

Then reality hits me and I can understand why he doesn't want our first time to be here on Riley and Char's couch. In fact, we're better off waiting until the time is right. I know that this isn't our first rodeo but I know it's going to be amazing. The longer we wait the better it will be; I just need to keep reminding myself of that.

I quickly pull myself together and gather my thoughts. I get up from the couch and call Manny back into the kitchen.

He follows my every move and sits down next to me with his tail wagging.

"Stupid dog," I mumble under my breath while picking up his food and water dishes.

"Hey, is that any way to talk to a family member?"

I turn around to see Pete laughing at me.

I look down to the dog and give him a genuine pout.

"Sorry, Manny, I'm just slightly bitter at the moment."

I watch as his ears perk up and I let out a laugh.

Scratching behind his ears, I watch as his leg starts to go nuts thumping on the tile floor.

"Belle, you're so cute when you're bitter," Pete says with a hint of humor in his voice.

"I'm even cuter when I'm….oh, never mind," I say, turning away from him.

I blow a strand of hair out of my face and move toward the pantry to get Manny some food. Pete comes up behind me and grabs the water bowl from my hands.

"Here, let me help you. The faster we get out of here the sooner we get some things done today."

I look over to him as he turns on the sink and fills Manny's bowl.

"What kind of stuff do we have to do today?" I ask, leaning up against the countertop.

"Well, for starters, we both need to go home and get cleaned up," he says, looking at his outfit and then mine. "We're still in the same clothes we've been in since yesterday."

I lift my arm to pretend I'm smelling my armpit.

"Nope, I'm still good."

He looks at me and laughs.

I stick my finger in my mouth and slowly pull it out.

"Yup, I even taste good," I say with a giggle as Pete drops Manny's water bowl in the sink and tackles me to the ground.

He starts to tickle me and I can barely breathe I'm laughing so hard.

"Okay, okay, please stop. I'll be good, I promise."

He stops tickling me for a moment and leans down to kiss me.

"You're going to kill me, little lady."

I lift my head to kiss him on the lips and squirm out from underneath him. I get up off the floor and walk over to the sink, fill up Manny's water bowl and set it down on the floor for him.

Standing back up, I look over at Pete who's now standing alongside the refrigerator.

"Okay, how about if we do this. We can both go home, take a shower and get dressed. When you're ready, you can come back to Derrick's and get me since his house is on the way to the hospital. We can go check on Riley and Char and then have the rest of the night to ourselves. Sound good?"

He walks over to me, wraps his arms around me and pulls me in close to him.

"I like the way you think, Belle, especially the part when we get to spend the night alone together."

"Me, too," I say, standing on my tip toes to kiss his lips.

He swats me on the ass and pulls away.

"Manny looks to be good here, let's get a move on."

I walk back into the living room, fold up the blankets and put the pillows back in their place. Everything else seems to be in order as I look around the downstairs of the house.

"Okay, I'm ready," I say, walking toward the front door.

Pete grabs my hand and we walk out the door and down the front porch steps to his truck.

"I'll be back in an hour, is that enough time?"

"Yep, I'll be ready to go."

He leans down to give me a heart stopping kiss and gets into his truck.

I stand and watch as he pulls out of the driveway and down the road. After a few moments of staring out onto an empty street, I pull myself out of my Pete daze. I hop in my car and head down the street to Derrick's house.

Opening the garage door, I see that his car isn't there. At least I won't be bothering them while I get myself ready.

I head into the kitchen and make a mug of coffee and quickly eat a bowl of oatmeal with a banana. I clean up my breakfast dishes and head up the stairs to take a quick shower. While getting myself dressed I hear the doorbell ring and rush down the stairs.

I open the door and there stands Pete in all of his handsome glory. Just the sight of him sends my senses into over drive. His bright blue eyes are looking down at me and I so badly want to jump into his arms.

Resisting my gut reaction to him, I step aside so he can come in. Even though I saw him less than an hour ago, I realize I've missed him.

"I'm almost ready; I just need to put on some socks and shoes."

"No worries, Belle. Go ahead and finish getting ready; I'll stay down here."

"You can come up to my room and wait for me if you want," I say, starting to walk up the stairs.

I stop midway when I notice he's not behind me.

"Aren't you going to come up?"

"Yeah, that's probably not a good idea. If I get you anywhere near a bed, we're not likely to leave the room for the rest of the day."

My cheeks begin to blush at the thoughts and images that immediately flood my mind.

"You're probably right. I'll be back down as soon as I can."

Oh my God, this man knows exactly what to do to affect me. I can't wait to have him all to myself later tonight. To be honest, I don't know where I plan to start with him, but once I'm done every inch of his body will be covered in trails of kisses from my lips.

Pete

I wait while Emma goes back upstairs to finish getting ready. I wasn't joking with her when I said it's best I stay downstairs. God only knows what I might do to her if we're alone in a bedroom.

The sexual tension between us is getting intense to say the least. I don't know that I have the willpower to stop myself the next time I'm on top of her.

I pace the kitchen for a few minutes and then a brilliant idea comes to mind.

I take a seat at the kitchen table and scroll through my contacts. I hit send on the one number and wait until she picks up the line.

"Hey, it's Pete. I need a favor for tonight around seven o'clock….."

"There will be two of us….."

"I want you to put out your best for me ….."

"Thanks….."

Well, that was easy. I guess it really *is* good to know people in high places. I've had this favor in need of a return and tonight is the perfect opportunity to cash it in. We'll need to do some errands beforehand, but we should have plenty of time.

I want to make sure Emma will have everything she needs for our night out together.

Hopefully, Emma will be surprised; I think this is something she'll like.

I want tonight to be a night Emma will never forget. I think it's going to be perfect.

I hear her coming down the stairs and watch as she rounds the corner and sits down on my lap. She wraps her arms around my neck and places a gentle kiss to my lips.

"I'm all set. You ready?"

"Yep."

"Okay then, let's roll," she says, hopping off of me and walking toward the front door.

I grab onto her hand and we walk out of the house and down the front steps.

"I'd offer to drive, but I know how much you love riding in the Mini. Oh wait, you've never taken a ride in my car."

"Belle, as much as I'd love to ride in the Mini, I don't think it was made for my six foot plus frame."

I watch as she lets out a giggle.

"Okay, tough guy, let's take the macho truck," she says, sticking her tongue out at me.

Dear God, between the way she looks at me with her eyes and the thoughts going through my mind of her tongue, I'm lucky if I don't bust a load in my pants right now.

"Let's go, shorty," I say, swinging my arm around her neck and pulling her into a head lock.

We make our way over to Massachusetts General Hospital and up to the ICU. Once we reach the right floor, we find the rest of the family in the waiting area sitting around talking.

"Hey guys," Emma says, walking toward Derrick. "Have you heard anything?"

He stands to give her a hug and reaches his arm out to pull me into a hug as well.

"Nah, not really. She still hasn't woken up. The good news is that the doctors are happy with her scans and the neurological tests they've done, but we need her to wake up to know more."

"At least there's good news coming out of all of this," Emma says, pulling away.

"Yeah, I know. It's just all the waiting that sucks."

I watch as the family interacts and discusses the things that they'll need to do for Char while she's in the hospital.

Each of the family members have agreed to take turns staying with Riley around the clock. Teresa has already contacted Char's employer to let them know what's been happening and Emma said that she'd take care of Manny as long as needed.

This is a strong family that will do just about anything to help someone in need. I've known just about all of them for years, and to be honest, they're the closest things to a family that I have here in Boston.

I just wish there was something more I could do to help.

Emma starts to scan the room, waves to the rest of the crew and then takes a seat next to Derrick.

"So, where's Chloe?" she asks.

"She just went in to see Char. Riley's been hogging up all of the visiting hours with her and they'll only let one person in at a time. He should be coming back out soon."

Just as Derricks finishes his sentence, Riley comes walking into the visiting area.

Emma stands from her chair and walks over to him. She wraps her arms around him as he pulls her into his embrace with his good arm.

"You doing okay?" she asks him.

"No, this fucking sucks. I keep talking to her, telling her how much I love her and need her to wake up. She's still knocked out; I just want my girl to open her eyes."

Riley looks over to me and nods his head to say hi.

"Riley, you know Char; when she's good and ready to wake up she will," Emma says.

"Yeah, that's what everyone keeps telling me. I just hate this waiting shit."

"I know. Is there anything I can do to help?"

"Nah, Derrick and Chloe brought me some clean clothes and Bryce and Teresa have been keeping me fed. How's Manny?"

Emma lets out a laugh and looks toward me.

"What's so funny? What did you two do to my poor dog?"

"We didn't do anything to him, it's what he didn't let *us* do," I say, pulling Emma into me.

"Shut the fuck up. *You two?* You didn't….not in my house….did you?"

"No man, your house is clean. No worries," I say with a laugh.

"Manny is good. Pete and I let him out and fed him last night and this morning. I'll keep an eye on him for you for as long as you need."

"Thanks, guys, we really appreciate it. Just don't be doing any funky business in my house. That's just gross," Riley says, running his fingers through his hair.

"No worries, little brother, anything we can do to help just let us know."

He looks like absolute hell and it's evident that the stress of Char is wearing on him. At least Emma and I were able to get him to smile for a few short minutes. It has to be hard. The waiting must suck for him. I can't imagine the pain he's going through sitting next to the girl he loves, knowing there's nothing he can do to wake her up.

Chapter 30

Emma

Pete and I spend another hour or so at the hospital and then decide to head out. I feel bad for leaving, but there really isn't anything we can do but sit and wait like the rest of the family.

Riley and Derrick promise that they will keep us up to date with any news on Char. I give everyone a hug on my way out and Pete wraps his arm around me as we make our way to the elevator.

"You okay, Belle?" Pete asks, pulling me into him.

I look up and give him a half smile.

"Yeah, I'm fine. I just wish Char would wake up. I feel for Riley and I hate that he has to be in so much pain right now. Is it wrong that we're leaving?"

He leans down and kisses my forehead.

"You're such a good person, Emma. We can stay as long as you want to, but all we'll be doing is sitting and waiting."

"I know; it just sucks for my brother."

"It does, but we have to stay optimistic and hope for the best. Char is a fighter and when she does wake up she's going to do everything she can to get her ass home to Riley."

"Yeah she will and I'll help her in any way I can."

"We all will; it's one of the things that makes this family so great. They're always willing to help and support one another."

The elevator stops on the first floor and the doors open. Pete grabs for my hand and we walk through the lobby of the hospital and out to his truck.

"Do you have anything you need to get done this afternoon?" he asks.

I stop in my tracks and look at him. "I don't think so, why?"

"I have a little something planned for us, but I wanted to make sure you didn't have anything you needed to do before I steal you away for the rest of the day."

It's still pretty early in the afternoon and I'm not quite sure what he has up his sleeve.

"Hmm, what kind of plans did you have in mind?"

"Don't you worry about what I have in mind, just do me one favor."

"Of course, what is it?"

A huge smile comes to his face.

"You have to do whatever I say, no questions asked and no arguments."

I laugh out loud.

"I have to do whatever you say and give all control over to you? I don't know what you have going on in that brain of yours, but I trust you enough to do whatever you want me to do."

"That's my girl," he says, opening up the passenger side of the truck and letting me in.

I watch as my guy shuts the door and walks around the front of the truck.

I don't know how or why he came into my life, but I'm so happy he did. He makes me feel so special. He treats me like I am the only person in the whole wide world that matters to him.

I smile at him as he slides into his seat and reaches for my hand. Staring into my eyes, he brings my hand up to his lips and places a gentle kiss on it.

My heart melts when I'm around him.

He lets go of my hand and starts up the truck.

"So, our first stop is to get our wardrobe for tonight," he says, looking in the review mirror and backing out of the parking spot.

"Ward—..."

"Ehh," he says sticking his finger up at me. "No questions allowed. You said you'd do what I said."

I cross my arms over my chest and stick out my bottom lip.

"You're cute, Belle, but I'm not falling for the 'pity me' look."

I let out a heavy sigh and watch as he starts to laugh.

"You'll love it, I promise."

"I know, I'm just playing with you," I say with a wink and a smile.

"Okay, then we're off. Sit back and enjoy the ride."

I lean my head back onto the seat and watch as we travel through the streets of Boston. Pete steers the truck onto a street that looks all too familiar to me. It's the place where Char took me the day after I arrived.

I'm not quite sure what Pete has planned for us, but shopping at Newberry Street is always a good idea in my opinion.

This place is a shopaholic's paradise; there are eight blocks of amazing stores.

"I want you to find something nice to wear for tonight."

"Okay," I say, giving him a questionable glance. "Can you tell me what kind of outfit I should be looking for?"

"Yes, a dress," he says grabbing for my hand. "I'll go first so you have an idea of what I'll be wearing."

"Sounds good."

We walk along the streets for a few minutes until we get to Alton Lane.

I've never been in this store, but I've heard about it and these people don't play around.

Pete opens the door for me and we walk inside.

We are immediately greeted by a female salesperson that starts asking Pete questions and I have no clue what they're talking about. She leads us over to a sitting area and Pete asks me to take a seat while he gets fitted, whatever that means.

After a few minutes Pete and the lady come back over to me with a few items. Pete walks into the dressing room and a couple of minutes later comes out wearing the most amazing suit I've ever seen on a man.

It could just be that it's Pete wearing the suit, but holy shit he looks hot. I stand from my chair to get a better look at this incredible man standing before me.

His suit is charcoal, with a light blue dress shirt that makes his eyes pop and a grey and blue stripped tie.

I move my hand to my mouth for fear that it's hanging open or that I might be drooling.

"You like it?"

"I think like is an understatement. You look amazing, Pete."

"Perfect, I'll take it," he tells the lady as he heads back into the dressing room.

Once he comes out, she properly hangs and folds his items, asking Pete to follow her up to the register. I wait for him by the door, and when he's ready we walk out of the store and back onto Newberry Street.

"It's your turn now, Belle," he says, leading me down the street.

I look in a few windows to find the perfect dress for tonight.

Stopping dead in my tracks, I've found it.

I pull Pete into the Crush Boutique and walk straight over the black cocktail dress I saw in the window. It's perfect. I look through the rack for my size and grab the hanger.

"I'll be right back," I tell him as I walk toward the dressing room.

As I put it on I feel amazing. The dress fits my petite body perfectly and accentuates the little bit of curves I have to my body. This is the dress that will make Pete's mouth drop and drool all night long.

I walk back out of the dressing room with my dress in hand and head toward the registers.

Pete meets me as the cashier is ringing up my purchase and insists this is his treat for me.

I'm in complete awe of him and can't wait to see what else he has in store for us today.

Pete

So far, we're off to a good start. Both Emma and I have chosen our outfits for this evening. Now all I have to do is get her back to Derrick's place and get ready without attacking her.

I pull into the driveway and help Emma carry our bags into the house.

"I'll get ready in Derrick's room and meet you downstairs once you're all set."

She gives me a smile and I can only imagine what's going through that pretty little head of hers.

We make our way upstairs and I quickly get ready. It doesn't take me long, but to pass the time I start to pace around the room. I'm excited and nervous about tonight. I've never put so much thought into planning a date before. I want Emma to know that I cherish her and that she means the world to me. I open the door to Derrick's room and start to walk down the hallway when I hear Emma open her door.

She stands before me in an amazing black dress that fits her tiny frame like a glove. She looks fucking hot as hell and is wearing a pair of heels that make her legs look unbelievable.

"Does this suit your request for wardrobe this evening?" she asks.

"Belle, we need to leave now," I tell her as I start to walk down the stairs.

"Pete, you're crazy, but I love it."

"We may be dressed for a night out, Emma, but I cannot *wait* to get you out of that dress later tonight."

She lets out a giggle and pulls herself against my body.

"We really should get going; I have reservations for us at six and I know we'll hit traffic heading back into the city."

She nods her head and follows me out the front door.

We arrive at Ristorante Toscano shortly before six o'clock. I watch Emma as she takes in the ambiance of the restaurant and the owner greets us at our table.

"Well hello, Pete, it's so good to see you again," Francesca says to me.

I stand from the table and pull her into a hug. "Francesca, this is my girlfriend Emma. Emma, Francesca's brother recently worked with the team on a new business he's planning to remodel uptown."

Emma gives Francesca a smile and extends her hand. "It's nice to meet you."

"If either of you need anything please let me know. We've prepared a spectacular menu for you this evening; I do hope you enjoy it."

"I'm sure we will. Thank you so much."

She walks from the table and I turn back to my girl.

"This place is beautiful, Pete," she says, taking my hand in hers.

After a few moments, our first course is brought to the table.

"I hope you're hungry."

"Actually, I'm starving," she says.

Throughout our meal, I watch Emma's expressions, her body language and her reactions during our conversations. I'm becoming more anxious as we near the end of our meal. I want to take her home with me so badly; it's beginning to drive me nuts.

After we finish the last of our meal, I lead Emma out of the restaurant and back out to the truck.

The drive to my house is only twenty minutes, but I felt like it took us twenty hours. I pull the truck into the driveway and rush to the passenger side of the car to get my girl.

We walk toward the front of my house hand in hand and I can almost feel the nerves we both feel pulsating through our hands. I open the door and we walk inside. Without a word, I lead her through the house and up the stairs.

As soon as we reach the top of the stairs I feel Emma pause.

"You okay, Belle?" I ask, turning to face her.

She nods her head and smiles back at me.

"Pete, I just want to thank you for today; it was absolutely amazing."

"Today, tomorrow or ten years from now I'll always do what I can to make you happy, Belle."

"You make me happy every day, Pete. You have no idea how much you mean to me."

"I think I do, Belle, now let me show you."

I take her hand and lead her into my bedroom.

I pull her into me and capture her mouth with mine. There's no hesitation as our tongues begin to touch and savor one another.

I reach behind her and begin to pull the zipper down her back, allowing her dress to fall down her body. Her perfect body is completely naked in front of me.

She stands on her tip toes and pulls my jacket off of my shoulders and lets it fall to the floor.

I pick her up and carry her to my bed. Hovering over her body, I lean in to kiss her softly on the lips.

"Emma, you are so beautiful. I will never take a day for granted that you are mine."

I run my lips down her neck as I lick and suck below her ear. I treasure her as I continue to kiss and nip down her body to her breasts.

"Pete, please," she cries. "I need you now."

I run my hands down the sides of her body and touch her most sensitive spot. I can feel her wetness and how ready she is for me to make her mine.

I push myself off of the bed to stand and look down at this woman lying before me. I quickly remove my tie, unbutton my shirt and remove my pants. As I start to remove my boxer briefs, she sits up on the bed and watches as I pull them down and allow them to drop to the floor.

I hear her breath hitch and there's no denying that we are both ready for this moment. I reach into the side table next to the bed and pull out a condom. I look into her eyes and she reaches her hand out to take it from me. She carefully tears the package, and as I kneel onto the bed, she pulls it down my length.

I move my body over hers and kiss her with all the love I feel for her.

Slowly and gently I ease into her warmth, not wanting to take this moment too fast. She rakes her fingers down my back and I rock into her a bit deeper. Once she's taken me in, she wraps her legs around my hips and I begin to make love to her. Our rhythm is perfect; it's like nothing I've ever felt with another human being. There is no doubt in my mind how much I love my Belle and I'm finally about to show her.

Epilogue
Four Months Later
September 2013

Emma

The past few months have been a compete whirlwind in the lives of my Boston family.

I busy myself in the kitchen preparing the food for our barbeque. Everyone should be here in the next few minutes and I can't wait to spend Labor Day with our close knit group.

It amazes me how far we've all come since I first moved here several months ago. If someone were to tell me that I was going to be as happy as I am right now, well let's just say I may have kicked them with my pointy hooker boots.

I'm happier than I've ever been and I can't thank Riley and Char enough for pushing me to move up here. This place, although scary and intimidating at first, is now my forever home. Moving in with Derrick was interesting to say the least, but now he's one of my nearest and dearest friends. Pete came into my life when I needed him the most. He's the man I've looked for my entire life and didn't realize even existed until I saw him that first night at Derrick's house.

Together, the six of us have experienced loss, heartache, second chance love and a rekindled romance. We've been there for one another through it all and I honestly don't know what I would've done without them.

We have so much to be grateful for and I know there are only better things to come in all of our lives.

A lot has changed since that night I spent with Pete. It's a night that I will remember as long as I live. Not just because it was the first time we made love, but it was the night we experienced the start of our lives together. Pete is my soul mate, my best friend and the man that loves me for who I am. He has seen me at some of the lowest points of my life, but no matter what emotional state I'm in, he's there to pick up the pieces and make me whole again. He's touched me in a way that no one else ever has—mentally, emotionally and physically. I never knew I could feel so connected to another person. I've realized just how much someone can mean to me since I've met him and he doesn't let a day go by without telling me how much he loves me. He cherishes me, nurtures me and always puts my needs before his own.

Things got a little crazy after the accident with Riley and Char. We all stood by Riley's side as he watched the love of his life lie in a hospital bed. There wasn't much we could do to help either one of them, but the day Char opened her eyes was one of the happiest days of my little brother's life. It was a struggle for a while until Char was able to come back home, but after numerous therapy sessions, she was back home acting like the tough cookie we all know and love.

As for Chloe and Derrick, their love was apparent from the moment I saw the two of them back together. Chloe went to her final interview with the Red Sox and kicked some serious ass earning a position on the media team. I don't know who was happier: Derrick at having his girl back in Boston or Riley knowing that he'd have season tickets to his all-time favorite sports team for life.

Pete and I talked about the idea of me moving into his house with him. I was a bit hesitant at first and scared to take that leap in our relationship. I waited for a few days before making my final decision, but I knew in the back of my mind what I really wanted to do.

Spending time with Pete is something I've enjoyed doing since before we entered our committed relationship. It was a no brainer that we were meant to be together, and as much as I told myself that I was scared, he'd eased my insecurities. He truly is my better half and I don't want to spend a day not being by his side.

We've all experienced a lot together, and no matter what life throws at us, we're right there to help and support each other.

Riley has been holding onto the engagement ring he bought for Char, but won't tell us when or how he plans to propose. I don't know if he's scared because of what happened the last time with the accident, or if he's just waiting for the perfect moment.

Chloe threw us all a curve ball by proposing to Derrick on the pitcher's mound at Fenway Park. To this day, Derrick raves that it was the best proposal he's ever heard of, but I think he's slightly biased. The girls and I have been running around like chickens with our heads cut off trying to organize their wedding that will be taking place in the next few months.

So much has happened, but I can't imagine any of our lives to have taken any other path.

As I set out the side dishes and fill a plate with food for the grill, I feel Pete come up behind me as he wraps his arms around my body. We may have fought the shock factor, but I can still always sense when he's near me. I don't have to see him or hear him to know when he's close to me; I can just feel his presence.

He leans his head down next to mine and peppers kisses along the side of my face.

I squirm in his arms as he begins to laugh.

"Can I help with anything, Belle?" he asks, turning me in his arms.

"Nope, I think I'm all set," I say with a smile.

"You really went all out today. Look at all this food. Are you planning on feeding our entire neighborhood?" he asks, leaning down to place a soft kiss to my lips.

"Ha, you're funny. You know how you guys eat. I didn't want us running out of any food. Plus, Derrick called this morning to say that Bryce, Teresa, Bud and Rose are coming, too."

"Okay, sounds good to me. The more the merrier."

I step up onto my tip toes and kiss him.

"I love you, Pete."

"I love you more, Belle."

I lean my body into his as he kisses me. I can never get enough of him.

A knock sounds at the front door and I hear everyone as they start to come in the house.

"Hey guys," I say as they start to walk into the kitchen.

Pete and I break free of one another and I start to hug everyone as they walk in.

"I brought wine," Char says, lifting up two bottles of our favorite white merlot.

"I brought dessert," Chloe says, setting down two plates of goodies onto the counter top.

I watch as Riley looks around the room and shrugs his shoulders.

"I brought an empty stomach," he says and we all start laughing.

"Come on, guys, let's head out back and we can get the grill started," Pete says, grabbing three beers from the fridge and heading out back.

"Our parents should be here soon," Chloe says, reaching for a carrot stick.

"I'm so glad they all decided to come," I reply, taking a seat on a stool.

"Me, too," Char and Chloe say in unison.

The three of us start to giggle and begin to munch on the snacks I've laid out.

The doorbell rings and I hop off the stool to get the door.

"Hey, guys, so glad y'all could make it."

They all walk through the door and greet me with hugs and more plates of food.

"You guys didn't need to bring anything, we've got plenty," I say, leading them into the kitchen.

"We couldn't come empty handed and I know how much Riley can eat," Teresa says, pulling her girl in for a hug.

"The guys are out back meddling with the grill. You're more than welcome to stay in here and chill with us girls or go out and show them how to man the grill."

"I'll show them how it's done," Bryce says, giving Bud a nod to follow him out back.

I look around the kitchen and smile.

Chloe is right, with all of our busy work schedules it's rare that all of us can be in one place at the same time.

I couldn't be happier to have my forever family here with us today.

Our barbeque is a success, not that I had any doubt. We eat, drink and talk about all of our plans for the rest of the year. Chloe stresses that we still have quite a bit to do for the wedding and I know that Pete wants to make a trip home to his sister for the holidays. The next few months may be jam packed, but I wouldn't have it any other way.

Just as the girls and I finish cleaning up the kitchen, Pete comes in to let us know Riley built a fire in the pit out back. We grab our glasses of wine and head outside to be with our guys. Together, the ten of us sit in a circle and enjoy one another's company.

Pete wraps his arm around me and I scoot in closer to him.

He whispers in my ear, "I love you, Belle. Thank you for making me a bigger part of this amazing family."

I lean into him as he grazes his hand along my cheek.

Never in a million years would I have thought I'd feel like this again. Pete has been the man who has listened to my cries, wiped away my tears and cared for me before I ever knew how much he meant to me.

I look into his eyes and see the man I've been waiting for my entire life.

"Thank you for loving me, but I love you more."

I'm no longer scared of where this will go; I can now say that I've been touched by another.

The End

Touched By Another Playlist

Permanent by David Cook

Slipped Away by Avril Lavigne

Stronger by Sara Evans

Irreplaceable by Beyonce

Take Care by Rihanna and Drake

The Finish Line by Train

The Only Exception by Paramore

Who I Am by Nick Jonas

You and Me by Lifehouse

Lucky Strike by Maroon 5

Fallin' For You by Colbie Caillat

Two is Better Than One by Boys Like Girls

You Found Me by Kelly Clarkson

We Belong Together by Gavin DeGraw

Everything Has Changed by Taylor Swift and Ed Sheeran

Bless the Broken Road by Rascal Flatts

Changed By You Between the Trees

Near To You by A Fine Frenzy

I Feel Like That by Jason Walker

Publishing Schedule

Touch Me August 26, 2013

Touched By You October 26, 2013

Touched By Another January 26, 2014

You've Been Touched February 14, 2014

Pierced Love December 15, 2013

Cursed Series Spring 2014

Fighter Series Summer 2014

About the Author

t. h.snyder is my pen name.

I am a 34 year old single mother to our two amazing kids.

I became an avid reader in spring of 2012 and since have read over 250 books.

My genre of interest ranges from Romance to thrilling Paranormal.

This is more than just a hobby for me, it's a passion to read the words of great authors and bring life to their stories with my reviews and character castings.

I started writing my first novel in June of 2013 and I am anxious to see where this journey takes me!!

You can continue to show your support by liking and following me on facebook, twitter, and goodreads.